The only word to describe him was *tempting*

David's hair still glistened from his shower as he went to the armchair and led Janina gently to the ottoman in front of it. "Lean back and I'll dry your hair like I used to," he said.

Janina knew it wasn't a good idea, but felt powerless to resist. She settled against him, into the space between his thighs, and was warmed by the heat of his body. He unwrapped the towel on her head and began a slow sensuous massage that electrified her nerve endings until she was almost hypnotized. But somewhere along the way David's touch grew bolder, and she felt his arms around her, his lips brushing her hair, her face, her brows.

David turned her face to his and murmured against her mouth, "We could be more comfortable in your bedroom."

ABOUT THE AUTHOR

Phyllis Taylor Pianka began her career in the arts as a self-taught painter of murals for public buildings in Illinois. When her husband was transferred to California, she indulged her lifelong affinity for writing. After one month she sold her first story; she has now had ten novels published, in addition to numerous short stories and articles. Phyllis has lived in Wisconsin, Illinois, Florida and Pennsylvania and currently makes her home in Cupertino, California, with her husband of almost forty years.

MIDSUMMER MADNESS

PHYLLIS TAYLOR PIANKA

Harlequin Books

TORONTO • NEW YORK • LONDON
AMSTERDAM • PARIS • SYDNEY • HAMBURG
STOCKHOLM • ATHENS • TOKYO • MILAN

To my husband, Ed, with love
To Don Carlson, for his inspiration
To Ruth Cohen, my agent and Debra Matteucci, my editor
with sincere appreciation and affection.

Harlequin Intrigue edition published April 1985

ISBN 0-373-22016-2

Chapter One

Janina Scott frowned as she glanced at the clipboard. The new patient was due up from Recovery in a little while and she wanted to talk to Dr. Clark about the case. There was something wrong there. She believed in facts...numbers. They were solid and dependable if you learned to recognize what they were saying. These numbers spelled trouble. She knew it as surely as she knew the physical layout of the hospital.

Janina took pride in her chosen career as patient coordinator at Mercy General Hospital. She had to. For the past three years her world had revolved around the inner workings of the hospital. Most of her friends were either on the nursing staff or in the administrative branch, and ninety percent of their conversations involved medical problems.

There was a time three years ago when it was different. When David was here. But he was married now, and things would never be the same. She had tried to accept it and was only now beginning to make a life for herself without him. It hurt. Time was supposed to heal everything, but no one had told her it could take so long.

She saw her reflection in the window as she passed

the central supply room and turned to go upstairs. Time had been gentle where her face was concerned. At least she had that to be grateful for. There were changes in her appearance, of course. She had cut her below-the-shoulder-length, gold-brown hair to form a cap of soft waves around her face. Not as romantic-looking as it used to be, but it was easier to care for and more appropriate to her age.

She smiled, remembering her friend Casey's reaction to that, and reminded herself that twenty-six was not exactly ancient, even though it seemed that way sometimes after a difficult case.

An orderly who stopped to let a wheelchair patient admire the view of the Santa Cruz Mountains caught her smile and returned it twofold. They exchanged greetings and Janina had the distinct feeling he'd like to get better acquainted. It was comforting to know that she wasn't completely over the hill. That was the trouble with broken relationships. It was apparently inevitable that you lose a certain amount of personal esteem along with the person you cared for.

But it was time she stopped mourning for what she had lost. It was time to expand horizons, get to know some people outside of her own little circle. After all, she reminded herself, this was California, land of fun in the sun. It was a shame to let it go to waste. She ought to plan to spend the weekend with her parents and her sister, Debbie. It had been nearly a month since she had driven up to Castro Valley to see them and she missed their company.

Now that her father had turned part of his produce business over to a new partner, her parents were enjoying the additional time they could spend together. They had begun taking day trips to such places as

Sacramento to see the fabulous Railroad Museum and the Winchester Mystery House in San Jose. At seventeen, her sister Debbie was old enough to stay alone, but they were cautious where Debbie was concerned. She was extremely pretty, and equally as free-spirited. For sisters, their natures certainly were different, Janina mused. Right now it seemed as if Debbie was headed for trouble.

With effort she pushed the thought to the back of her mind and braced herself for a verbal duel as she approached 309 West. Vince Costello had made it a point to get the best of her ever since he was brought into the emergency room at Mercy Hospital three months ago. Often as not he succeeded. She embarrassed easily, even after four years of active nursing followed by two years at her present position in administration at Mercy Hospital.

The curtain was drawn around his bed and she looked at her watch. "I see you're busy, Mr. Costello. I'll come back in a half hour and help with the insurance forms."

"That you, Scotty? Come on in. You can finish my bath."

"You need my help like you need a wig," she said, thinking of his mop of woolly black hair.

"Hey, a blond wig might be a good idea. They say blondes have more fun."

"If you had any more fun, you'd be spending the rest of your life in the hospital. Finish your bath. I'll come back later."

"Listen, don't go for a minute. I hear I'm getting a roommate. Is she young and available?"

"He's middle-aged and very sick, so behave yourself. His name is George Murdock. He'll be coming up from Recovery in about an hour."

"What's wrong with him?"

"He had surgery of the pancreas. Look, go easy on him, Vince. You about drove poor Mr. Lidell crazy."

"Pete Lidell was already crazy. Did you get a look at that wife of his? She must have kept him broke buying dog biscuits."

"Vince, I'm warning you."

She heard him chuckle and it was a good sound. There had been a time when he was in Isolation that they didn't think he'd make it. Now his burns had begun to heal and the pain was manageable, but just barely. He used humor to combat depression.

"You still there, Scotty? I said I'll behave if you'll make it worth my trouble."

"Sure thing. I'll take you on a field trip downstairs for a barium enema."

"Thanks for nothing."

"Don't mention it. Get on with your bath. I'll see you later."

Her smile was genuine as she left his room. Sometimes she missed nursing. It was grueling, dirty work. Heartbreaking, too, when you lost a patient you had come to care for. That was one of her problems. She had cared too much and a nurse couldn't afford that luxury.

In the few years she had spent in bedside nursing, there were dozens of cases she remembered. The ballerina, Sarah Noland. A courageous woman who had never once complained despite the pain she had suffered after she lost her leg to gangrene. The Major...she never could remember his name, who had tried to take over the entire third floor and run it like a battalion of infantrymen. It had taken one of the orderlies, Johnny Granger, an ex-GI, to make him settle down and accept orders from the staff. Then of course there was the teenage boy, Billy Merchant, who nearly lost his leg to infection before she and David saved him. It was the catalyst that brought David and Janina together, but she didn't want to think about it now.

Health care was like a revolving door. New faces, new problems, but always the same demands on time, energy and emotions. It wasn't an easy life, but she loved the hospital atmosphere and would be lost without it.

As she walked down the hall, her thoughts went back to the new admission, George Murdock, who had just come out of surgery early that morning. Another case of pancreatitis. What was going on, anyway? When she had voiced her concern at a staff meeting two days ago no one had been perturbed, but in the four years she had served as a nurse she had taken care of only a handful of acute cases. Now they had... what was it, three in one week?

Casey Walters waved at her from the nurses' station. "Got time for a coffee break, Janina? Somebody brought in a sack of doughnuts from the Nut Hut."

Janina smiled at the plump redhead. "I'll take time. It's been a long day and my feet feel as if they've been cast in concrete."

"I thought only fat people like me got sore feet." She shoved her pen in her pocket and put the chart into its metal folder. "My day has hardly started. God, I hate three-to-eleven," she said as she tried to match her short legs to Janina's long stride. "You were smart to get out of nursing. What I wouldn't give for a nine-to-five job."

"Come on, Casey. You know you'd miss all this."

"Yeah," she agreed as she opened the door to the nurses' lounge. "The lavish furnishings, the sumptuous decor."

Janina grinned as she looked around the tiny cubicle, which nearly bulged with two plastic club chairs and a sagging sofa. They were grouped around a coffee table that held the tape recorder used for reports, and a collection of outdated magazines scrounged from the visitors' waiting room at the other end of the hall.

"You're right. We need to do something about this mess. Maybe I can bring it up at the next staff meeting."

"Forget it. It keeps us from loitering too long on break. So what's in the wind these days?"

Janina shrugged. "Not much. I'm still keeping an eye on the nurse down in Physical Therapy. But don't you dare let that get passed around."

"Safe with me."

"Good. It helps to have someone to talk to. We go back a long way."

"We do, don't we? Sometimes it seems like a lifetime ago when we signed up for training at San Jose Hospital. Then again, it seems like yesterday. Funny. We both swore we were gonna travel around, see some of the country, but we both ended up here in Willowbrook, a ten-minute drive from San Jose. I'm not sorry, though. My kids love it."

"There was a time when I wanted to leave but . . ." She shrugged. "I don't know where I'd go."

She thought about it some more as Casey devoured a doughnut. Except for the fact that it was a company town, Willowbrook wasn't bad. It was just an hour or so to San Francisco, an hour to get to the beach, less than that to get to the mountains to enjoy a picnic in the woods. The Tahoe ski area was only a few hours' drive to the northeast. In short, it had everything. She was born in California and she suspected she would be content to live the rest of her life there.

When David first left, Janina had wanted to leave town, start over, do anything to fill the empty spaces he had made in her life. It had taken the first few months for the numbness to wear off. After that, she became so engrossed in her work that there was no time to go through the ordeal of resettling in another town. Besides, her family wanted her close by. And so she stayed.

Casey looked at her curiously. "I thought for a minute I'd lost you. Sure you don't want a doughnut? I'm going to have another before I go back to face the screaming hordes. Lordy, if we have to admit any more patients, we're going to have to put them in the hall stations."

Janina passed up the doughnut. "Casey. Have you noticed anything unusual about the number of acute pancreatitis cases that came in this week?"

"Well, now that you mention it, it is kind of odd. I can't ever remember having more than one on the floor at a time. Half the time the suspected cases turn out to be polyps or an ulcer, anyway. Why? What makes you ask?"

Janina shrugged. "I don't know. It's just that I have this feeling that—"

The beeper interrupted her and she pushed the button down to stop it. "That's my office. Sorry. I guess I'd better check in and see what's up."

"Sure. I'll walk you partway to the station. More than five minutes of this unadulterated luxury is too rich for my blood. Let's get together some night as soon as I get back on day shift and we'll do the town. You know, find us a nice singles bar and..." She saw the expression on Janina's face. "Yeah...yeah. I know you hate bars, but maybe we'll get lucky and meet some nice guys. Or are you still dating our good Dr. Morrison?"

"Off and on, but neither of us is serious. Steve is fun to be with and certainly good-looking, but he's a little too smooth for my taste."

Janina had first seen Steve Morrison around the hospital but she didn't get to know him until one time at the local country club they were paired off for mixed doubles in a charity tennis tournament. He had taken her out to dinner afterward and somehow they fell into a dating routine that had lasted nearly a year. But it had held no excitement for her, even the dinners at the club or the dancing at the Fairmont in San Francisco.

Janina thought about it for a minute. "Steve is all right, but there's no special chemistry between us. He's a social climber and you know how I feel about that. Anyway, I'm just not interested in dating right now."

"Listen, kid. You've been saying that for a couple years."

Janina made a face. "I guess so. Half the time I take a stack of work home with me and I keep so busy I don't have time to think about finding a man."

"Well, think about it. These are supposed to be our prime years!"

Janina smiled and waved as she continued on alone to the telephone at the nurses' station. It *had* been a long time since she had dated seriously. Sometimes she yearned for the warmth of shared companionship, the feeling of being close to someone who cared not just about physical desires, but emotional needs as well. But when David left, it was as if she closed off a certain part of her mind; the part that meant home, family and togetherness. In the meantime she dated when it was convenient and it was more than enough for her at the present.

"All right if I use the phone, Ellen?" she asked the floor nurse, who nodded permission.

"Janina Scott. You have a message for me?"

The operator paused for an instant. "There's a man waiting to see you in your office, Janina. No appointment, but he said he'd wait. He was rather insistent... in a nice way. I can tell him you're busy, though, if you'd rather."

"No. It's all right. I'm finished up here for now, so I'll go right down. Thank you, Carla."

It was still visiting hours and the elevator was crowded as she got on and told the man nearest the control panel that she wanted the main floor. Several people stopped her as she cut through the lobby to the C corridor where her office was located. She encountered families of most of the patients at one time or another in her capacity, and many of them remembered her. Usually, it was a question of helping them understand the rights and responsibilities of a patient or simply assisting them as they filled out application forms for insurance or disability payments.

Once in a while, though, her duties placed her squarely in the middle, between patient and staff. That's what was going to happen with Nurse O'Connor down in Physical Therapy. There had been stories, mostly second- or thirdhand, of her threatening some of the patients with violence if they refused to do the prescribed number of exercises or follow their diet to the letter. As if they weren't already traumatized simply by the separation from their families. Assuming the stories were true, the woman was a psychological menace and Janina had to find out the truth behind the stories before someone got hurt. Most nurses were above reproach, but once in a while one slipped through the screen and presented the hospital with a problem.

She sighed and smoothed the skirt of her periwinkle-blue suit, wondering about the man waiting in her office. *I hope it's something simple,* she thought. It had been a long day and she wanted nothing more than to go home and relax.

DAVID MADISON RAN HIS FINGERS through his thick dark hair in a characteristic gesture of frustration. He stood slowly, unused to sitting for so long, and walked across the teal-blue carpet to study the picture on Janina's desk. Older man, woman and young girl. Her father and mother and her sister. Debbie was her name, wasn't it? He felt a surge of hope. If Janina had married, she would have had her husband's picture on the desk. She must still be single. When he learned she was still using the name Scott, he had begun to hope, but now his hope grew stronger. *Dear God, let it be so,* he thought.

It had been three years since he saw her that last time. It was the day he told her that he and Susan were going to be married. The look on Janina's face had nearly been his undoing, and the memory of that day still had the power to cause him pain.

Leaving her was the hardest thing he had ever done.

In the eight months they had dated, they came to know each other as well as anyone could, short of marriage. Rather than breeding contempt, as the saying went, familiarity had drawn them even closer together.

Being a nurse, Janina had understood his inflexibility when it came to putting the good of his patients first. She had forgiven his lack of mechanical skills, and she overlooked his tendency to be compulsively neat. Her flaws, on the other hand, were few and far between. He found them charming, rather than irritating. Besides, the things they had in common far outweighed their differences.

They both loved the woods and the water more than they enjoyed man-made activities, except for music. And they both loved to eat. He chuckled now as he thought of the meatloaf she had prepared in a pressure cooker. It was blood-red when it was finished. She tried to feed it to the cat, but even she turned up her nose. They had settled for McDonald's.

There was an elusive something about Janina that had attracted him from the first day he saw her at the nurses' station in the Intensive Care Unit. She was efficient; he liked that. She moved gracefully, with gentleness and an economy of motion that gave her a heightened aura of femininity.

He reached into his suit jacket and extracted a worn photo of Janina perched on a rocky outcropping at Land's End. Her hair whipped in the breeze like a dusky gold mane, and her T-shirt clung to her breasts like gift wrap on a birthday present. Moments after he snapped the picture, a wave had drenched her. She wasn't angry, but she wasted no time in making sure that he got as wet as she was.

What was she like now? Had she changed? He had

been forced to wait three years to come back to her. But the waiting was over now. Susan was dead, had been dead for nearly five months. And for the first time in a very long time he was free, really free.

David turned as he heard the door open. His heart gave a sudden lurch as he saw Janina standing there so slim and lovely. She had matured during those three years. *And God help me,* he thought, *she's more desirable, more beautiful than I could ever have remembered.* She had cut her hair. No longer the shiny golden-brown mane that hung to her waist. Now it fluffed around her face in soft, glossy waves. Even her eyes had changed. They were still the clear blue of the summer sky after a shower, but they were less innocent, less trusting than he remembered. It hurt him to know that he was at least partially to blame for that.

"Hello, Janina," he said at last. There was a huskiness in his voice that surprised him, and he cleared his throat. "It's been a long time."

"David?" She shook her head as if to clear it. "I...I can't believe it's really you." *Oh God,* she thought. *Why are you doing this to me?* She had tried so hard to forget him, but hardly a day had gone by that she didn't remember. She could reach out and touch him now and her fingertips would recall the texture of his skin, the springy thickness of his dark hair and the way it grew in a swirl at the nape of his neck. She remembered the good clean scent of him when he had held her in his arms.

She moved across the room to the comparative safety of her desk, aware that his gaze all but consumed her. "You're looking well, David." *Liar,* she thought. He looks tired. Worn, like a fine oil painting that had suffered the passage of time. Tiny lines of worry etched his face and the youthful fire in his eyes had darkened to cobalt blue.

He moved toward her and she began to panic. "Sit down, David. Please," she said, motioning to a chair opposite her. Then she took her own place behind the desk.

He hesitated, then nodded and sank down slowly as if his mind was weary and preoccupied. *She's as nervous as a doe sniffing the air,* he thought, *and no wonder.* Aloud he said, "I guess maybe I should have called to let you know I was in town but I..." He smiled and shrugged. "I guess I'm a coward. I was afraid you'd refuse to see me."

She drew a deep breath and assumed her "hospital official" facade of unflappable calm. "Don't be absurd, David. Why should I do that?"

His eyes darkened and a look of unbelievable sadness crossed his face. "Janina Scott, don't play games with me. We've been through too much together to waste time pretending. Above all, we've always been honest with each other."

Her eyes sparked fire. "We've been honest? Then why do I have the conviction that this honesty bit was all one-sided?" She was glad for the excuse to be angry. There was safety in anger. "Face it, David. We were pretty well committed to each other, or at least that's what you led me to believe. Then, like that—" she snapped her fingers "—you dropped the bombshell that you were getting married the next day to your high-school sweetheart. If that's your version of honesty, then heaven help me."

He saw that her hands were shaking and the thought comforted him. She still cared enough to be angry. He leaned forward. "I told you why I married Susan. She was dying and she was alone and frightened. I was the closest thing to a relative she had, and I couldn't just pretend I didn't care. Sure, I could have had her put in a hospice, but that wouldn't have worked at all. She was too frail to be among strangers.''

He leaned his elbows on his knees and bent forward, running his fingers backward through his dark brown hair. "Good God, Janina. In many ways I loved Susan. I just wasn't *in love* with her the way I was with you. Can't I make you understand that?''

"Of course, the fact that she was very rich didn't hurt any, either.''

He was silent for a moment and when he spoke his voice sounded old and tired. "I wish you hadn't said that.''

Janina sighed. "So do I. But the thought did cross my mind and I've never been one to hide what I'm thinking. I'm sure you remember that.'' Her voice sounded strained, even to her own ears, but she forced herself to go on. "Tell me, how does your wife feel about this unexpected visit to Willowbrook?''

David held her gaze with his. "I'm confident she would be very pleased. Susan died of leukemia five months ago.''

Janina's face crumpled. "Oh, David, I'm so sorry. Forgive me. I shouldn't have. . .''

He gestured with his hands. "Don't. It's all right. This misunderstanding has been between us for a long time, and I hoped that you would see me again and we could talk it out.''

She laced her fingers together, feeling the bones through the tautness of her skin. "Three years is a long time, David. Maybe it's a subject better left alone. I've made a new life for myself since you moved back to San Diego. It doesn't include you.''

He rose and walked toward the window and for a moment stared unseeingly at the distant Santa Cruz Mountains, which ran like a narrow blue-gray ribbon along the lip of the horizon. In the foreground, liquid amber trees, heavy now with ripening burrs, dotted the lawn that gave way to city streets busy with rush-hour traffic from San Francisco.

Absently, he reached up to untangle the philodendron vine that hung from one of the ceiling hooks to form a shimmering green curtain against the July sunshine.

Janina remembered those fingers; fine-boned, clean-scrubbed, the hands of a skilled doctor. She could almost see the sun glisten on the gold-tipped hair that was sprinkled over the backs. Most of all, she remembered the way they felt against her skin. Strong but at the same time incredibly gentle as they moved her to unbelievable heights of passion. He knew how to please her and doing so had given him pleasure in return.

She stirred in her chair, hoping to ease the tension that was like a tangible thing between them. For once, she prayed for the phone to ring and break the spell, but it was stubbornly silent.

He cleared his throat and spoke, his voice husky. "I see you still like growing things around you. Do you still have your fish and your cat?"

She relaxed a little. They were on safer ground now. "Yes. I've bought a condominium, though. Cinnamon likes the patio."

"One of those chrome-and-glass creations over on Wellington?"

She smiled, knowing he didn't believe it for one minute. "No. I bought into The Willows over on Park Lane. Lots of glass, but it's redwood instead of chrome."

"Cozy."

"As a matter of fact, it is." They were marking time. She knew him well enough to recognize his tactics. When he was unsure of himself, he danced around a subject, approaching it from all angles until he had taken its measure and found the weakest point. Soon he would get to the real business at hand.

"Your place sounds nice. Will I get to see it?"

"I. . . No, David. I don't think so." He had startled her with the abruptness of the question. Not like him at all. He usually paved the way first instead of coming out with a bald statement. It was one more change she recognized in him.

She had once considered him the ideal man. At six feet he was the perfect height for her five feet seven inches. He was good-looking but not pretty, strong but not muscle-bound, firm in his beliefs but not totally inflexible. Perfect, almost. And maybe that was the problem. She had expected too much from him, counted too much on him to return the love that she felt for him. But Susan had held a special place in his heart and when it came to a decision, there was no contest.

"Janina." There was an urgency in his voice that tore at her insides. "Listen to me. I want to see you again. I need to. All these months I've been kicking myself for what I did to you. Wishing I could have married you instead of Susan."

"Great. That must have made Susan happy."

His voice hardened. "She was happy. In many ways Susan was a little girl. She lived for each day and the small surprises it brought. I did everything I could to make every minute of her life as wonderful as possible for her. But I didn't love her, Jan. Not in the way I love you."

The telephone shrilled for attention and Janina grabbed it like a blessing from some kindly providence before the first ring completed. "Janina Scott."

She listened for a moment, then told the doctor she would speak to the patient's family in a few minutes. Hanging up the phone, she turned to David.

"I'm sorry. I have to see some people on an urgent matter." She stood and walked around the desk as she held out her hand to him. "It's been good to see you, David. Please accept my deepest sympathy over the loss of your wife. Have a safe trip back to San Diego."

He reached for her other hand and held them both in his cool, firm grasp. "And that's all? Dammit, Janina. I didn't take a month off from the hospital just to hear you mouth some lousy platitudes. I'm not leaving until you promise to sit down and talk this out."

She tried to pull away, but he held her firmly. "Let go, David. You'll make a scene if they open the door."

"Good. Let's give them something to remember." He pulled her against him and kissed her harshly at first, but his mouth softened as he felt her tremble. "Janina, Janina," he murmured against her mouth. "Don't send me away like this. Not until we've had a chance to see if there's anything left of the way we were. Promise you'll give us a chance."

She tried to pull away, but he held her not ungently in the circle of his arms. It was impossible to ignore the pain she saw in his eyes, but at the same time her own pain was too fresh to be pushed aside so easily. "David, I can't. I swore I'd never be hurt again the way I was before."

"I'm not asking for anything more than you want to give. Just promise to talk to me."

"I have to go, David." His face lengthened in disappointment. Janina didn't want to hurt him. She didn't want revenge for what he had done to her, she just wanted him to leave. But the expression in his eyes told her that this time he would stay until they talked it out.

She relented, knowing it was a mistake to spend time with him. Just seeing him stirred memories that should have been forgotten, but she had little control over her emotions where David was concerned. It wasn't just that she wanted him to make love to her. Being in the same room with him, watching the way his mouth moved when he talked, enjoying their heated discussions, laughing at some silly joke...everything about him was dear to her. She pressed her palms together.

"I... All right, I'll give you an hour or so to say what you came up here to tell me."

"Tonight?"

"Yes."

"Your place?"

"About seven-thirty."

"Want me to bring something for dinner?"

"It wasn't a dinner invitation, David. We're just going to talk and then you're going back to San Diego and leave me alone."

"If that's the way you want it."

There was a knock at the door of her office, and David had the grace to leave without causing her further anxiety.

The couple introduced themselves as Laura and James Creighton, the parents of Michelle, a ten-year-old who had been brought in to the hospital three days ago with a persistent sore throat. X-rays had shown nothing unusual except for an advanced infection of the tonsils. A staff doctor recommended a tonsillectomy, but they had read that most tonsillectomies were inadvisable. They wanted an opinion from a doctor who was not affiliated with Mercy Hospital, but they weren't sure how to orchestrate the procedure.

Janina opened the drawer of her desk and withdrew a sheet of paper. "I'd like to give you a copy of 'The Patient's Bill of Rights,' which is put out by the American Medical Association. If you like, I can go over it with you point by point. In the meantime, we'll work out a procedure for bringing in an outside doctor to look at your daughter. I must warn you, though, that when another doctor is brought into a case, even from the same hospital, an additional fee is charged."

They seemed to understand. Since they had the name of a doctor who had been recommended to them, Janina helped them schedule an appointment for him to come in to do a complete workup on Michelle the following day.

It took her longer than she expected. The Creightons were extremely concerned about their daughter, an only child. Talking seemed to ease their fears, and Janina had developed the art of listening. It wasn't all one-sided. Hearing their problems helped her forget that in a little while she would be seeing David again.

Her car was parked in the lot nearest the emergency room. As she was leaving, Del Carnaby, the head nurse in ER, was holding the door open for the ambulance attendants.

Janina stopped to talk to her. "What's coming in?"

"I'm not sure yet. Ulcers, maybe. Acute abdominal pains, nausea, vomiting. Could be almost anything."

"Not another pancreatitis, is it?"

"Not very likely."

But Janina knew it was. She would have staked her

life on it. *Damn,* she thought. *Damn!* Maybe David would have some insight into the incidence of the disease. He was on the staff of a major hospital and he knew his business. *Admit it,* she thought. *You want to see him. You know you do. But be careful. You've got to consider the consequences before you reopen the door to the past. This time the hurt may go too deep to heal.*

Chapter Two

When Janina got home from work, David was waiting on the redwood bench by her front door, looking cool and virile in a blue polo shirt and white duck trousers. She experienced a wave of helplessness, of being caught up in a current too strong, too powerful to resist.

Her voice mirrored her anxiety. "David, you weren't supposed to be here until seven-thirty. It's just after six."

"I know. I brought some stuff from the deli. I knew you'd be too tired to cook, and if you did, you'd never be able to eat it." He grinned. "It's lobster salad. Want me to take it and go?"

She couldn't suppress a smile. "Oh, come on in. You're right about one thing: My cooking hasn't improved and I probably would have skipped dinner. I have the only cat in the world who likes her canned food better than people food."

"Smart cat." He looked at her bulging briefcase. "You always bring this much work home?"

"Usually." She shoved the key in the lock and opened the door. "The kitchen's to the right. You can put the stuff on the counter."

He came into the living room as she was sorting her

mail. It was a pleasant, contemporary room with polished walnut tables, pale-gold carpeting, a pair of beige love seats patterned with pale-blue irises. A lounge chair upholstered in blue velvet backed up against a wall of nubby beige draperies. The overall effect was soothing.

"Nice place," he said. "It looks like you, Jan. Did you do the decorating?"

"Most of it. I chose the colors and picked out the chair and sofa but had a decorator do the draperies and carpet because of my limited time. The kitchen's all mine, of course."

"You didn't have to tell me. Nobody but you would have green things sticking out of every nook and cranny."

At that moment Cinnamon, the reddish-brown cat that David had always claimed looked more like an Irish setter, poked her nose into the living room. Seeing that the coast was clear, she stretched her front end, then her hindquarters, laying her ears flat against her head in a motion that made her eyes slant upward.

Janina patted her hip, but the cat—stubborn as always—chose to go to David and rub her head against his leg. Janina swore softly. "Fickle female. Don't get bigheaded about this, David. Cinn takes to every man who walks into the place."

David studied her face. "And have there been so many?"

"That, my friend, is none of your damn business."

"You're right, of course. But can I ask this, Janina? Is there someone special at the present time?"

"No."

"No, I can't ask, or no, there isn't?"

"No, there isn't and I happen to like it that way."

He seemed completely undaunted. "Then what say I fix dinner?"

"Well, since this is your party, you take over the kitchen. As soon as I change clothes, I'll set the table."

"Just like old times?"

Her voice was steady as she leveled him with her gaze. "No, David. Not like old times. I told you before that I don't want to get anything started again and I meant it."

Nothing seemed to bother him. He simply grinned and said, "Put something on the stereo?"

She didn't bother to answer but went into the den and switched on the intercom. He no doubt expected her to play a Mantovani tape that they both had loved, but out of self-preservation she turned the stereo to an FM station that scheduled a program of semiclassical music.

Going into the bedroom, she hurriedly hung up a dressing gown she had left on the bed, then mentally scolded herself. Why should she care if the room was less than perfect? She wasn't about to let him go into her bedroom. Still irritated with herself, she went to the closet and selected a blue-and-white sundress and a pair of red sandals to put on.

It was still warm in the house, but rather than turn on the air conditioner, she opened the door to the patio, which was enclosed by a high stone wall. The muted tannish stone was softened by tendrils of variegated ivy spider-webbing its way across the far end. A tablecloth covered the picnic table where she often ate the few meals she prepared at home.

David made a pitcher of iced tea to go with the lobster salad. He had warmed tiny corn muffins in the microwave and they smelled heavenly. As they sat down, he squeezed lemon juice over wedges of freshly cut melon and enormous glistening red strawberries.

Janina felt her determination slipping. "You do have a way with the kitchen, David. I've missed your cooking."

"Among other things, I hope."

He watched her unfold the peach-colored linen napkin, which matched the curtains in her kitchen, and place it on her lap. His pulse jumped as irritation flickered across her face. Why couldn't he remember to go slow with her? If he rushed her, he could frighten her off for good.

She placed her fingertips in a straight row along the edge of the table and spoke quietly, without undue emotion.

"Don't try to move too fast, David. I have plenty of scar tissue to deal with. I'm not sure I care to expose all my old wounds. Believe me. At this point, I'm very much inclined to tell you to get lost."

He let out a deep sigh of relief. "All right. We'll take it slow, Janina. I've waited a long time for you. I'm willing to wait longer."

They ate in silence for a few minutes. Lobster was Janina's favorite food, but then of course David knew that when he was plotting to tempt her. She wondered if he remembered their three-month anniversary when he had taken her to San Francisco to the Lobster Grotto, where they had indulged in a lobster orgy. It was the most delicious meal she had ever eaten. Afterward, they browsed in the shops along Fisherman's Wharf and she bought David a dragon kite with a twenty-foot-long red tail. He bought her an alabaster egg.

When they went back to her apartment, they made love and talked about her family and his family and the family they would like to have. David's mother had died about six years earlier. His father was living in London, where he worked in an office of an international investment corporation. Although David and his father kept in frequent touch, they rarely saw each other and David missed having a home to go to. Perhaps that was why he had enjoyed Janina's family, Janina decided.

David was also remembering the day of the lobster, as they had come to call it, but he thought it wise not to risk antagonizing her. He looked up as he swirled his tea in the tall, frosty glass.

"What ever made you give up nursing to become a patient coordinator, Jan? It certainly came as a surprise to me. You were an outstanding nurse. It must have been a difficult decision."

She shrugged. "In some ways, yes, but it was either that or give up the health-care field completely. I had been working in Intensive Care for the last four years and I just couldn't take it anymore."

He nodded. "I've heard that for most nurses it's a toss-up between ER and ICU for a quick burnout."

"Emergency room's even worse, I think. I don't see how they handle the round-the-clock stress. As a patient advocate, I still work directly with the patients but I get to know the families, too, and I can be of real help to them. It's a darn good feeling."

She speared a strawberry and bit a small piece from the end. "Not only that. A patient coordinator working as a patient advocate has considerably more clout than a nurse, strange as that may seem. A nurse has to bow to the demands of doctors. I don't, thank God. Of course, I still have to answer to the board of directors and if I make a complaint I had jolly well better be right or I lose my credibility."

"It sounds like you've finally found your niche. No problems, then?"

"Heavens, I didn't say that! There are always problems with red tape and lack of space and money, but I can handle most of the situations. If I can't, I ask for help."

"And you get it?"

She stirred in her chair and leaned back to study a basket of fuchsias that cascaded in pink and purple splendor down to the floor. "I've always found help until now, but something's been happening lately that puzzles me."

He waited expectantly and she leaned forward to study his reaction. "What would you say if your patient load of acute pancreatitis changed from an average of one a month to three in one week? No, make it four. Another possible was just brought in as I left the hospital this afternoon."

He stroked his chin and stared into space as he considered the options. "It's a bit unusual. Pancreatitis is certainly ordinary enough. The majority of patients with acute pancreatitis have alcoholism or gallstones as an etiologic factor. Postoperative trauma is the third most important cause of acute pancreatitis, and I'm inclined to think that vascular insufficiency of the pancreas may be a more common cause of the disorder than we've been led to believe."

"And how about hereditary factors?"

"Familial pancreatitis can be inherited as an autosomal trait, but any other form of pancreatitis in children is extremely rare."

"Thank heaven we haven't had any admissions to Pediatrics. What bothers me is that from what I can tell, none of the pancreatitis cases appears to fit the norm. No alcoholism, no postsurgery cases... Something just doesn't jell."

He pushed his chair back from the table. "That does

seem strange. A total of four in one week, you say?'' He chewed his lower lip. ''Well, it isn't impossible, of course, but it is something to watch.'' He turned sideways and crossed his knees as he cradled the glass of tea in his hands.

''Listen, Jan. If you're trying to prove a case of misdiagnosis, I think you'd be wasting your time. The clinical presentation is quite clear-cut. As for the lab tests, the diagnosis relies heavily on the measurement of serum amylase.'' He took a sip of tea. ''Granted, an elevated level can be manifested in other conditions, but given certain symptoms, diagnosis is not that difficult.''

Janina shook her head. ''It's not a question of doubting the diagnosis. More than one internist is involved and they happen to be some of the most capable doctors on the staff. Maybe you remember Jameson and Pfeiffer. Peter Thomson is new since you left.''

He nodded. ''Good men, both of them. But if it's not the diagnosis, what's the problem?''

''Good question. I don't really know, David. It's just a feeling I have that there's more to this than just coincidence.''

He drew a deep breath before he spoke. ''At the risk of sounding condescending, aren't you perhaps borrowing trouble?''

''You mean you think maybe I'm taking my job as patient coordinator a little too seriously?''

''Uh oh. Do I detect a note of hostility?''

''Sorry. I didn't mean to be testy. After all, I did ask your opinion.'' She stood up and began stacking the dishes. ''I got the same feedback at a staff meeting, and it still smarts. Maybe I'm completely off-track, but it keeps eating away at me and I can't shake the feeling that we're missing something. I guess time will tell.''

He picked up the empty salad bowl and followed Janina into the kitchen. "Speaking of missing something. I don't suppose you have any of those lemon bar cookies your mother makes, tucked away in the freezer?"

Janina laughed. "As a matter of fact, I do. Mom keeps me well supplied and she'd be thrilled to know that you remembered them."

"I would be happy to tell her in person."

Janina drew back. "That sounds very much like a hint to me."

"Perceptive, as always."

"But not receptive, so save your breath, Dr. Madison."

"I have more where that came from. As I recall, your parents liked me quite a bit."

Janina leveled her gaze at him. "I've never denied, David, that you have a certain boyish charm that turns old ladies into giggling teenagers."

"Your folks approved of my taste in women, too."

"If you mean because you dated me. Yes, they approved very much at the time. I'm not sure how they would react to you now, though, considering everything." She looked away, settling her gaze on a pot of rosemary.

His voice softened. "I can understand that." He wanted to hold her, to comfort her and kiss away the hurt that he had caused. Instead, he reached for her hand and turned it over, tracing a line on the tender palm with the tip of his finger. "I'd like to be given the chance to rebuild my bridges."

She sounded bitter in spite of her efforts to keep her tone neutral. "Burned bridges can't always be rebuilt, David. Sometimes it's better to go in different directions." She withdrew her hand, missing the warmth of his fingers even before it was gone. But he wasn't to be put off.

"I don't give up easily, my friend." He turned his back to the counter and braced his hands against it as he watched her arrange the leftover muffins in a plastic container.

"You once told me I could put anything back together. Remember, Janina?"

She nodded. "The Henderson woman. She had been riding on the back of her boyfriend's motorcycle when he hit a bridge abutment." Janina's eyes shone as she faced him. "I saw Katrina a few months ago. What a joy she is. You'd never know to look at her that she had spent eight months in a wheelchair."

"You see?"

"Bones aren't the same as relationships, David. Feelings can run too deep for the surgeon's knife."

He turned to stroke the petal of a blue-and-white African violet that grew in the greenhouse window over the sink. "Then maybe surgery isn't the answer. Sometimes therapy works better."

"And sometimes it's better just to pull the plug and let the patient rest in peace."

"I firmly believe in the old adage 'Where there's life, there's hope.'"

Janina found it hard to conceal a smile. "But Franklin said, 'He who lives on hope will die fasting.'"

David grinned. "Okay, so you one-upped me. I'm not about to try to compete with your literary talents, but I promise you this: We belong together, Janina, and I intend to do everything I can to make you admit it."

"Don't expect too much from me, David. I still care enough for you that I don't want you to get hurt."

He grinned and Janina was surprised to see the lines of fatigue around his mouth erased. His eyes warmed with a welcoming glow.

"Hey...a seed of hope. That's more than I had any reason to expect. Considering your talent for making seeds grow, our prospects are limitless."

She laughed despite herself. "And you are an expert at spreading it." She tried to busy herself with rinsing the glasses. It would be so easy to fall back into their old comfortable rut. This time she couldn't afford to let it happen.

David studied the slim lines of her figure as she leaned over to run water into the sink. The blue sundress, with its edge of white piping on the bow, stretched snugly against her breasts, outlining the soft fullness. His fingers still remembered their texture, like warm, living satin. Once he had loved to watch them become firm and supple beneath his hands. The thought was unsettling. He took himself out to the patio and brought in the rest of the dishes.

"Do you still see your family frequently?" he asked.

"Not as often as I'd like to. It's just an hour's drive to Castro Valley, but I only get up there a couple of times a month or so. My sister Debbie comes down to spend the weekend sometimes, but things have been a little tense with her recently."

"Oh? Man trouble?"

"She's been running around lately with a fast crowd. I think they've been drinking a little too heavily."

"Maybe it's just a stage she's going through."

"Maybe."

He put his hand on her arm. "You're tired. Let me put the dishes in the dishwasher."

Janina shook her head. "No, thanks. You fixed dinner. I'll clean up. There are some *Natural History* magazines in the den if you want to look at them.''

A little while later, she went into the den and found David sound asleep in the lounger with Cinnamon curled up under his hand. The cat had missed David, too. Cinnamon was rarely impressed by Janina's visitors, but she considered sleeping on David's lap as the next best thing to having her own steak hot off the barbecue grill. Apparently his two-year absence was quickly forgiven. Janina wondered at her own lack of resistance where David was concerned. What was it about him that held such wondrous appeal to her?

She had first gotten to know him when he was on the staff at Mercy and she was working the night shift in ICU. Billy Merchant, a teenage boy, had been admitted with a severe infection of the left heel. There appeared to be a minute puncture wound, but the X-rays were clean. Within twenty-four hours the boy's temperature skyrocketed and gangrene had begun to set in. David was afraid they might have to amputate his leg.

Neither David nor the consulting physician could find the source of the infection, but David spent hours with the boy trying to find out the cause of the puncture. Then one night when David and Janina were alone with him, Janina persuaded the boy to tell the truth. He admitted that against his parents' orders, he had been skin diving near the pier and had impaled his foot on a catfish spine. Surgery uncovered a tiny spur that had traveled upward through the muscle tissue and was invisible to the X-ray. The boy recovered quickly. Within a week, he was the terror of the hospital.

But Janina and David were never quite the same after their shared experience. That night had been the beginning for them, and she remembered it as if it were yesterday. When she got off duty that next morning, he was sprawled across the hood of her Datsun, waiting for her.

"I think the two of us deserve a celebration, Janina," he had said. "Do you like the beach?"

"I love it."

"Why don't we pack a picnic lunch and drive to Carmel? I know an isolated cove where we can sit on the sand and watch the sea otters chase each other over the rocks."

She offered to fix fried chicken and he promised to take bread, wine and cheese. She should have known better. Cooking was a lost art where she was concerned. Even the sea gulls refused to eat her chicken. The crabs stole big chunks of it, but David swore they were simply burying it to get it out of sight.

She wasn't angry. She hated to cook. The incident cured her of making any future attempts at using him as a guinea pig.

Despite the chicken fiasco, the day proved to be enchanting. David tried hard to make up for his teasing. As they watched the crabs scuttle around the bones, he took her face in his hands and lifted it up to his.

"Look, Jan. The food isn't important. We have bread, a jug of wine...and each other. What more could we ask for?" He kissed her for the first time, softly, tentatively brushing his lips against hers until her mouth became soft and vulnerable. Then he took her in his arms and his hands moved down the length of her back, molding her against him until every fiber of her being, every nerve-ending in her body, came alive with a special awareness.

His tongue teased the corners of her mouth, then and as his kiss deepened, explored the sweetness within.

Their breathing had become rapid, and as Janina met his passion with growing excitement, she returned it kiss for kiss. He groaned softly in pure pleasure at her response. His thumb had discovered the soft underside of her breast, stroking it gently in ever-widening circles that radiated waves of heat through Janina's body.

In their splendid isolation, David had awakened a need in her that she had only sensed before then. She responded willingly, arching her body against his until her pulses throbbed and the very center of her being warmed like liquid honey. She opened her eyes to look at him, to engrave forever this moment in time.

He saw her watching him and smiled. "You see?" he murmured against her forehead. "We don't need food when we're here in our secluded cove with no one to see us but the crabs and the gulls."

"Um." Her voice was breathy. "And that crowd of school children climbing over the rocks."

He swore competently. "So much for deserted beaches."

As he rolled away from her, she dusted her palm across the fine, gold-tipped hair on his chest. "Lady," he whispered. "If you don't want me to give those children a very graphic lesson in sex education, you'd better be careful." He captured her hand and laced her fingers in his. "Want to go for a walk? I think I could use the exercise right about now."

He pulled her to her feet and they walked arm in arm along the tide line, picking up shells and smelling the strong, pleasantly pungent odor of kelp drying in the sun.

He had taken her home that night and fixed dinner for the two of them in her tiny apartment. It was three weeks later when they slept together for the first time that Janina at last discovered the true meaning of fulfillment. After that, they were together whenever possible and it was a period of euphoria for Janina. The only thing that made it better was when he suggested they think seriously about getting married before the end of the year. Whenever Janina caught the scent of seaweed drying on the beach, she thought of that day at Carmel.

It was a few days later when David broke the news about Susan.

Janina stirred in her chair. She had been listening to the stereo and watching David and the cat sleep. It occurred to her that David must have driven all the way from San Diego that day. No wonder he was exhausted. It was about an eight-hour drive.

The music stopped and an after-shave commercial blared into the velvet quiet otherwise unbroken but for the sound of the bubbler on the aquarium.

David woke with a start that elicited a reproachful meow from Cinnamon. "Oh, hell. How long have I been sleeping? This was supposed to be my big chance to talk to you, and I guess I blew it."

"It's all right. I've been sitting here thinking about some of the times we had together."

He yawned and leaned his head back against the chair as he studied her face. "Concentrate on the good times, Janina. There were so many of them. Sailing, horseback riding, driving up to San Francisco to the symphony concert whenever we could afford it. Did it ever occur to you, Jan, that we never ever had a really big confrontation?"

"Just the one. . . but that was enough."

"Can't we put it behind us?"

"I don't know."

"Will you try? I'd like to court you all over again—if you'll give me a chance."

Janina's body flooded with the warmth of sudden desire. She had known her answer the moment she first saw him standing by the window in her office. But prudence warned her to be cautious.

Her finger traced the welting on the arm of the chair. "We can see what happens." Then she looked up at David and a smile lighted her eyes. "If I refused, Cinnamon would never forgive me."

"Remind me to bring her a pot of catnip."

The cat heard her name and stretched out her front leg, then reached over to give her approval with a quick rasp of her tongue on David's wrist.

The commercial ended and the announcer came on with the nine o'clock news. Janina started to change the station, but David stopped her.

"Let's hear what the weather forecast is for the weekend. Maybe we can get in some sailing if you don't have anything important planned."

"I can't. I thought I'd drive up to Castro Valley on Saturday to see my parents and maybe try to talk to Debbie."

"We could go up together if you don't mind me tagging along."

"I'm not sure it's a good idea just yet."

"Okay. I won't push, but I'd like to get your family back on my side. How about if I send a bushel of peaches up to your mom? She used to love it when I did before."

She smiled. "Bribery would get you nowhere. Besides, we can't. They just started a quarantine because of the fruit fly. You can't take any kind of fruit or vegetable across the county line. Didn't you see the roadblocks on your way up?"

"I guess I did, but I didn't pay much attention. They're always fighting some kind of bug here in California; the white fly, the Japanese beetle, the gypsy moth. You name it."

"This time it's serious. They've even brought in teams to spray certain areas like they did a few years ago in Santa Clara County, for the Mediterranean fruit fly." The announcer intruded on her thoughts and she held up her hand. "Listen, they're talking about it now."

". . . and reports are just coming in that three more female fruit flies have been found in traps near the foothills area of Willowbrook. Harvey Rudolph of the Department of Agriculture informed us moments ago that emergency measures are under way to stop the spread of the fruit fly into adjoining areas. When asked if those emergency measures included aerial spraying of malathion, Rudolph gave a terse 'no comment.'

"Meanwhile, protest groups are gathering their forces to prevent the use of broadcast spraying by helicopters. More on the ten o'clock news."

Janina sighed. "Well, here we go again. I wonder if they will try to force everyone to pick all of their fruit and destroy it. When they had the Medfly, people actually came to blows over stripping their trees. For a while the county began to look like a police state, with neighbors turning in each other for not picking their apples, or taking a peach in a lunch bag across the county line."

"Sure, but if they didn't control it, the fruit fly could destroy the entire industry here in the valley. That has to account for millions of dollars."

"I know. But don't you get the feeling there's no end to it?"

David put the cat down on the floor and patted her haunches as she yawned and headed toward her food bowl in the kitchen.

"It's a fact of life and there's nothing we can do about it, I guess."

"That's my point, David. I hate being ineffectual."

"No one would ever call you ineffectual. We all have different areas of effectiveness, that's all." He leaned back in the chair and crossed his ankle over his knee. "Now getting back to your mother. If I can't send her a bushel of peaches, what could I give her that might make a good impression?"

"Your head on a silver platter, maybe."

"That bad, huh?"

Janina nodded. He blew his breath out through his mouth.

"I knew this was going to be rough, but I can see I have a lot of explaining to do."

"Not tonight, though. You need to rest, David. You look done in."

His eyes twinkled with amusement. "It's early. I haven't even seen the rest of your house."

"You saw the bathroom. There's only the bedroom and storage room."

"I'll pass on the storage room."

"Weren't you able to get a room at a motel?"

"As a matter of fact, not yet. I saw a couple of signs and there was no vacancy."

"Oh. Well, don't worry about it. I have a few connections and I can get a room for you at the Presidential over on Market Street in five minutes."

His voice was dry. "Speaking of ineffectiveness! Somehow I knew you could handle it."

She smiled bewitchingly. "And since you have your

car and you know the general layout of the town, it shouldn't be any problem for you to find your way over there.''

"That sounds like my exit line." He put his hands on her shoulders. "Then the least you can do is to give me a proper send-off."

His gaze held hers for a moment and as he lowered his head, Janina closed her eyes and yielded herself up to the warmth of his mouth. He smelled of soap and expensive after-shave. Another change. In the old days he couldn't have afforded it. His hand cupped the back of her head and the disturbing thoughts began slipping away like so much spindrift left on the beach after a sudden storm.

She loved the way his fingers moved across her back, their caressing warmth permeating her clothing. Her own hands found their way around his waist, linking together behind him, drawing him close. Her body remembered as if it were yesterday, instead of two years ago, that she last had been in David's arms. The missing years served only to heighten her need. Her breath quickened. The warning echoing in her head sent waves of caution to her sensitized body.

"I think it's time for you to leave, David."

"Just saying good night, Jan."

"Um. In braille? Come on, I'll walk you to your car." She drew away reluctantly and he offered no further argument.

The air was heavy with the scent of jasmine. Over by the pool someone had tuned a radio to a big-band station and the music wafted pleasantly across the grounds. A man jogged by and said hello to Janina. David looked at her with a question in his eyes, and she laughed softly. "A neighbor, that's all." And then it was quiet.

There were two cars parked in the visitors' section. Without thinking, Janina turned toward an older-model Pontiac. He took her arm.

"No. It's the Mercedes."

She felt a cold shiver run down her back. *Susan's money again. Damn!* How many other changes had she wrought in his life? Would David's wife always be able to insinuate herself between them, even after death?

He put his arm around Janina and rested his chin on the top of her head. "I'll see you tomorrow."

"No. I have to work," she said. Her words were frosted with ice.

He held her at arm's length. "What is it, Janina? You've pulled back into your shell."

She shook her head. "Forget it. I'll work it out. And I have plans for tomorrow night, so don't ask."

"Cancel them."

"No. I can't do that."

"Can't?"

"I don't want to, David."

He just nodded, then got into the car and closed the door. He sat looking at her for a breathless moment, then started the car and shoved it into reverse. Another minute and he was gone.

Janina wrapped her arms around herself in spite of the warmth of the night. It surprised her that he had given up so easily, but it was better this way. Where David was concerned, she sometimes lacked the power of her convictions. Better to end it before it got started again.

When she got back to the house, Cinnamon had curled up in the chair that was still warm from David's body. Cinnamon had her own basket and Janina didn't encourage her to sleep on the furniture, but Cinnamon had always been crazy about David. Maybe the scent of him still clung to the chair.

"Traitor," Janina whispered, stroking the cat's head. Cinnamon was in no mood to be bothered. She tucked her head beneath her front leg and settled down for the night.

THURSDAYS WERE ALWAYS BUSY at the hospital and Janina was grateful that this was no exception. She didn't want time to think about anything but her job. Even so, whenever a group of nurses and nursing assistants congregated, the only subject under discussion was whether or not the county would force everyone to pick the fruit from their yard gardens. The prune plum trees were loaded this year and in about two weeks they would be ripe.

"I'll be darned if I'm going to waste all that fruit this time," Martha Crossman said. "Last time, they told us we'd be fined if we didn't pick them, but my neighbor had prunes, nectarines and everything, and she didn't get fined."

"I would have turned her in," Virginia, the floor nurse, said.

One of the nursing assistants whispered behind her hand, "Virginia would turn in her own grandmother." She laughed at her own joke and started coughing so hard she nearly choked.

"Damn!" she said when she could catch her breath. "It's that malathion they use to spray for the fruit fly. I don't know what they put in it, but it sure gets to me."

Virginia sniffed. "Of course, the three packs of cigarettes you inhale every day doesn't have anything to do with it."

"That's all you know about it, Virginia," one of the

nurses said. "I hear that the environmentalists have petitioned Judge Thorpe to write a restraining order to prevent any more spraying. They say it's giving a lot of people headaches and respiratory problems."

Virginia pushed her glasses back onto the ridge of her nose. "People are like sheep. They follow the leader. If the media didn't keep dredging up horror stories that have no basis in fact, there wouldn't be so many psychosomatic illnesses. Isn't that right, Janina?"

"Don't ask me." She laughed. "I took down my shingle a long time ago and I'm not going to get caught in the middle." She waved as she went toward the elevator.

The rest of the morning was taken up with family interviews. The worst, or at least the most difficult, of them came when she talked to a woman whose husband was near death from an automobile accident. She needed counseling on how to go about donating his organs to needy recipients. Janina found it to be the most traumatic of anything she was ever asked to do and yet the most rewarding. Months later, family members often came to her and told her how grateful they were to be able to enrich another person's life. She tried to keep that thought in mind during the interview.

A check with ICU gave her the first lift of the day. The patient who had been brought in to ER the night before had a perforated ulcer. The number of pancreatitis cases was back to three. Not that it made it any easier for the patient. Janina was just glad to have a brief reprieve from her concern over the increase in pancreatitis cases. Maybe whatever it was that caused them had run its course.

Before she left work that afternoon, she picked up the box of chocolates one of her patients had given her and took it up to Casey Walters. She looked as if she needed something. Her red hair was sticking out at odd angles from under her nurse's cap and there was a faint sprinkling of perspiration on her turned-up nose.

"You have time for a break, Casey?" Janina asked.

"No way. I just got word from Admissions that they need two more beds. Looks as if we're going to have to set up some hall units."

"Accident victims?"

"Observation. At least they're ambulatory."

"Well, thank God there haven't been any more pancreatitis patients admitted today."

Casey gave her a queer look. "Then you haven't heard. Another case came in this afternoon. It's only a probable. They won't know for sure until they get the results from the serum amylase. The woman is Dr. Morrison's patient." She closed her report book and slanted a look up at Janina. "Didn't you say you have a date with him tonight?"

Janina's pulse jumped. "Damn," she whispered. "I knew it. This is it. I've had it." She smacked her fist against her palm. "Excuse me, Casey. I've got to run."

She knew Casey would think she was crazy, but if she didn't get out of there she was going to burst. She had to find Steve Morrison before he left the building. At least he would listen to her.

Chapter Three

It wasn't difficult to find Steve. He was alone in the doctors' lounge, going over charts. His English-tailored suit, neatly buffed nails and carefully styled brown hair attested to the fact that he was a very successful doctor. He was going places in his chosen career and he had mentioned more than once that if Janina stuck with him, she could follow him right up the ladder.

He was smooth, no doubt about it, but contrasting him now with David, Janina wondered what she had ever seen in Steve Morrison. She greeted him with what she hoped was a show of confidence.

"Steve. You're just the one I was looking for. I heard that you have a new admission who is a pancreatitis probable."

He looked up, then looked quickly back at his notebook. "Uh-huh. I hope you're not going to get started on that epidemic kick that you dredged up at the staff meeting."

She noticed for the first time the hard edge of his mouth. "Steve, listen. You *know* there's something strange there." She leaned toward him and put her hand on his arm. "Look. If you don't want to get involved in it, how about letting me look at the patients' records? Maybe I can find something that ties them all together.''

He swore softly as he got up. ''I can't do that. Listen, you keep this up and you're going to get kicked out on your ear.''

''It's not exactly a criminal offense, Steve. All I want to do is see the records.''

''Who the hell do you think you are? Some kind of detective? Stick to your insurance papers and your release forms, Janina, and let the medical personnel handle the treatment aspect. There's nothing worse than an ex-nurse who comes into a position of authority.'' He put his hand on her knee and squeezed. ''Come on. Why so serious? Take off a little early. You should be on your way home to make yourself beautiful for our date tonight.''

She looked down at his hand and was revolted by his attempt to put her down and by his unexpected sudden intimacy.

''I'm sorry, Steve. I don't think I can make it. I've had a long day. Would it be an inconvenience if I begged off tonight?''

His lower lip pushed out over the upper one. ''Well, I did plan to take you to the club for dinner but if you would rather not—''

''Thanks. I really would prefer not to go out tonight.'' Before he could say anything else, she walked out and closed the door softly behind her. That was it. She was finished with him. . . . And damn, it felt good. One way or another, though, she was going to have a look at those charts.

FOR ONCE SHE WAS ABLE TO LEAVE the office a little early. When she got home, David's Mercedes was parked in the visitors' space. He was sitting inside. When she pulled her car into the reserved space, he got out and waited for her to come toward him.

She didn't want to see him tonight. Her resistance was low and she didn't want to have to be on constant guard against her feelings. He must have been in a good mood; humor sparkled in his deep blue eyes and around the generous curve of his mouth.

"We didn't make it clear whether your date was for dinner or if you were planning to go out later."

"No. We didn't."

He looked disappointed at the hint of irritation in her voice. "Care to elaborate?" She didn't answer and when they reached her front door, David rested his hand on the frame and propped himself against it.

"Not that I'm trying to be pushy or anything. I thought maybe I could interest you in a couple of egg rolls and some almond chicken and sweet and sour broccoli. Just in case you need to fortify yourself against this guy you're going out with."

"Not tonight, David. I have a lot to do."

"Yeah. Your date."

"No," she said before she had a chance to think, and immediately regretted it. She sighed in irritation. "As a matter of fact, I'm staying home tonight."

He grinned. "You broke your date to please me."

"Oh, David. You're insufferable. I did no such thing."

"But you'll invite me in."

"Not tonight."

She was having trouble fitting the key in the lock, and he took it from her hand and opened the door.

"Okay, Janina. I don't want to bore you. I can tell you some other time what I found out about the new pancreatitis admission at City Medical Center."

"What?"

"I had a feeling that might get your attention."

"All right, David. This had better be the truth. Come into the den and sit down."

He leaned back in the chair, looking smug and relaxed. For a moment Janina thought he was bluffing, then he linked his hands behind his head and caught his lower lip between his teeth. She held her breath until he spoke.

"Notice now," he cautioned, "that I'm not agreeing with your theory that we might have the beginnings of an epidemic here in Willowbrook. But since I had some spare time, and motels can be very boring, I decided to go over to City Medical and see what their census is like."

"And?" She was sitting on the edge of her chair.

"As of last week, they have three confirmed cases of acute pancreatitis." He held up his hand. "Wait now, before you get too excited. At least one of them is an advanced alcoholic and another is post-op, so it doesn't support your theory one way or the other."

"And the third?"

"Middle-aged man, general good health, no obvious trace of alcoholism, appears to be in the primary stage of the disease. That's the best I could do."

"How recently were they admitted?"

"The first two, at the beginning of the month. The last one, just this week."

"I guess it might be difficult to draw a parallel among the three cases." She told him what had happened at the hospital that day. "But I can't get anybody to listen to me. They simply aren't convinced that the cases are more than coincidence."

"They could be right, you know."

"I don't believe it for one minute, David, and you wouldn't either if you were still on the staff at Mercy."

"So what are you going to do about it?"

"I don't know, but I've got to find out the truth one way or the other. I'd like to get hold of the patients' records and see if there is some thread that ties them together."

"You'll have to have permission from the attending physician—"

"Or from the patients themselves. It could cause a lot of trouble. Word has already gotten around about the fuss I raised at Staff."

He nodded. "You could jeopardize your job. Why don't you get their names and addresses first? That shouldn't be too hard. Then we can take it from there."

"We? That sounds like you plan to help." It was hard to believe that David was going to support her in this, but the warmth of his gaze was encouraging, even if he was only doing it to placate her. She spoke softly. "Then you really do think this is more than just a flight of my imagination?"

"It deserves looking into."

Maybe he was being evasive, or maybe he was simply being cautious, but whatever his motive, she was glad to have someone to talk to about it.

He stood and she was impressed with the way his tan gabardines complemented his muscular thighs and trim derriere. He chuckled as if he knew what she was thinking, and she could have kicked herself for being so obvious.

"You look hungry, Jan. Maybe we'd better do something about that."

She saw the expression in his eyes and instinctively

backed away. He started to laugh, then looked at his watch. "I was talking about food, love. We could concentrate better if we had something to eat first. My Mercedes is going to smell like the Golden Pagoda if I don't bring in the carry-out stuff I bought for dinner."

She smiled slowly. "I think I could manage a pot of instant rice, if you're brave enough to risk it."

"Great. And put on some water for tea."

"You really are eager to live dangerously, aren't you?"

They spent a pleasant evening together. Janina was on guard against any romantic advances that David might make, but he didn't once try to touch her. It was a little disappointing. The old David would have been more aggressive. She found herself wondering over and over if he was more disciplined or simply less interested in making love to her. She knew she should be relieved to be able to relax and not fight him off, but some perverse side of her nature wanted him to prove that he still wanted her, whether or not she wanted him. By the time he left, she was mentally exhausted.

Janina could hardly wait to get to work the next day. After making sure that only those people who needed immediate help were scheduled for appointments, she checked the admissions sheets, then made the rounds of those patients who were listed as having pancreatitis. It wasn't likely their doctors would complain if she merely visited them. She had mentally prepared a list of questions in the hope that the answers would reveal certain similarities in the case histories.

By the time noon hour rolled around, she had talked to the pancreatitis patients who were well enough to be questioned but had not uncovered a single similarity. David stopped by to take her to lunch at the Critical

Care Bar and Grill, where many of the hospital people took their noon break.

It was much the same as he remembered it; a casual, red-checkered-tablecloth kind of place with silk rosebuds in a bud vase on each table. At night the vases were replaced with net-covered red globes, each holding a candle that sputtered and sparked. They sat down at a table in the far corner, next to a row of ruffle-curtained windows that looked out over a small courtyard.

"You look depressed," he said as he sprinkled pepper on his turkey sandwich. "Nobody said we were going to find out anything the first day. Hell, maybe there isn't even anything to find out."

"But I thought there would be something to tie them together; a restaurant where they ate, some medication they were taking. . . even their ages or their occupations. But they're as different as. . . as egg roll and T-bone steak."

He studied the crease that had begun to form between her eyes and he wanted to smooth it away. . . to assure her that everything would be all right. But he knew she was too smart to be treated like a child. "You ready to give up, Janina?"

"No. I can't. Not yet."

"So where does that leave us?"

"All I have left is their home addresses."

"Well, that's something. Do you have a recent map of the city?"

"No. There is one down the street at city hall. I saw a big one on the wall in the lobby when I went there to check on my listing in the city directory, and I think they have them for sale in one of the offices."

"Do you have time to go now?"

She looked surprised. "Yes. I'll take time. Right now it seems to be my only lead." She studied his face. The tiny squint lines by his eyes made it look as if he were laughing at her. "David, you aren't doing this just to please me, are you? I don't want to be humored like a stubborn child."

He reached over and took her hands between his. "You are every inch the woman, Janina. Haven't I always treated you as one?"

She knew what he was thinking and she blushed. "Hurry up and eat so we can go to city hall."

CITY HALL WAS only a few blocks away, and they chose to walk. Willowbrook was a garden city, full of open spaces where trees and flowers grew among exquisitely manicured lawns. Industrialized though Willowbrook was, most of its industry dealt with computer design and software, or otherwise "clean" manufacture. The larger buildings were set back behind man-made mounds landscaped with fountains, streams and small bridges tucked into the pathways at interesting angles. The willows for which the city was named had long since given way to easier-to-care-for trees that were more ornamental. The brook was still there, but it had been cemented high on each side to prevent flooding during the winter rains.

Janina enjoyed walking beside David. Her long legs matched his stride. She was sometimes uncomfortable walking with shorter people, but he was the right height for her and she knew they complemented each other in appearance.

As they approached the stucco-and-glass building, David stopped at a newsstand and picked up a paper.

"Well, Judge Thorpe did it. He wrote a restraining order against spraying for the fruit fly."

Janina breathed a sigh of relief. "Thank God. Maybe the malathion doesn't hurt anything, but I've been wondering about it lately. Look how much they used to spray DDT. It took them years to find out the horrendous consequences of that."

David shrugged. "I'm not so sure I agree. True, DDT proved to be a real threat, but the tendency is for the environmentalists to find fault with anything that smacks of progress. Even the number of cars on the street. But they'd be the last ones to give up their big cars."

"Speaking of cars, the parking lot is jammed. It's a good thing we walked."

"City council meeting, maybe?"

"I doubt it. They usually hold them at night to give the public a chance to attend. You know, the 'government in the sunshine' idea."

David held the door, then followed her into the wide lobby of city hall. The receptionist's desk was vacant and a sign attested to the fact she would return in ten minutes. Janina turned toward the left corridor.

"I guess we'll have to wait until she gets back to buy a map, but we can look at the one on the wall opposite the council room."

Their footsteps were loud against the marble floor. The huge map was extremely detailed.

"You have the list of addresses?"

"Sure," she said as she drew a notebook from her handbag. "Fullerton Street is the first one. I think it's in the foothills area east of town. 10729 is the number."

David took his pen from his jacket and used it for a pointer. "Right. The one-hundred-seven block is way out, almost at the end. What's next?"

"Mesquite."

"Here it is. Only a block long, and it's in the same area."

Janina heard the interest begin to build in his voice. "How about 10532 Juniper?" she asked.

"Two blocks from Mesquite." As he turned to look at her, a uniformed guard opened the door to the council room and a sudden hush fell over the crowd of fifteen to twenty men as they looked out at David and Janina.

David whispered softly, "Will you get a look at all the blue suits. It looks like bankers' day."

The mayor was sitting at the head table, and Janina saw him nod toward the officer, who closed the door abruptly before approaching David.

"You folks have a problem?"

"None at all. Just looking up a street on the map."

"We'd appreciate it, sir, ma'am, if you'd move along. You're disturbing the meeting that's going on in council chambers."

Janina smiled up at the guard. "Sorry. I thought we had been rather quiet. What meeting is it?"

"I . . ." He apparently wasn't prepared for the question, but he quickly recovered himself. "The library commission."

Janina was angry at the bold-faced lie. "Really. That's going to come as a big surprise to Margaret Childers, the chairwoman."

The officer visibly tensed. "Why don't you two just step into the room next door and we can discuss it?"

David grabbed Janina's arm and steered her toward the front entrance. "Thanks, officer. We wouldn't want to disturb anyone, would we, Janina?"

Fortunately, they were outside before she had time to tell him what she thought.

"Did you see that?" she snapped. "He was going to question us, wasn't he? Damn! I feel like a criminal and I haven't done anything yet."

David winced. "That 'yet' bothers me. What have you got in mind?"

"There's something fishy going on here, David. I'd bet my money on it. Tell me I'm not crazy."

"If you are, we're two of a kind. One of those men used to be county health commissioner, but I can't remember his name." He looked at his watch. "You're going to be late for work if we don't hurry."

Suddenly the thought of going back to work was very depressing. She sighed. "I'll never be able to concentrate on insurance forms and Medicare information. What are you going to do this afternoon?"

He shrugged. "I have a stack of medical journals with me that I need to catch up on. I was hoping you could have some time off and we could do something together. Go sailing, take in a matinee in San Francisco, visit the aquarium. The choice is yours."

"I can't. Especially not now. The hospital is overcrowded, and besides, I want to keep my eye on things."

He thought he heard genuine disappointment in her voice and it gave him the courage to ask. "Want me to cook dinner for you?"

"No, David. I don't think so."

He shrugged. "All right. I'll see you later."

THE REST OF THE AFTERNOON was a series of minor frustrations. At three o'clock David called. "Are you alone?"

"Yes, at the moment."

"I've been thinking, Janina. Has it occurred to you

that the pancreatitis incidents began about the time that they started spraying for the fruit fly?''

She made a sound in her throat. "I...the thought crossed my mind. I've been afraid to say it. It sounds so unbelievable.''

"Well, get this. I bought a city map, and all of the cases center in the foothills area where they have an abundance of home orchards. Better yet, that's where the county has been concentrating its spray campaign.''

Janina felt her skin turn cold and goose bumps prickled her arm. "Then that's it! It's the malathion that's behind the increase in pancreatitis.''

David hesitated. "I don't know, Janina. It sounds too pat. I think we need more proof.''

"Proof, hell! We can't wait around for other people to be brought in with the disease. I'm going to see the hospital administrator right now.''

"Maybe you should hold off a little, now that the judge has declared a moratorium on the spray campaign.''

She wavered. "I don't know, David. I just don't know what to do." He didn't interrupt her while she thought it over. Then she spoke reluctantly. "All right. I'll wait. But listen, if you hear anything else, be sure to call. Okay?''

"Sure.''

After she hung up the phone, she went over their conversation. David was right. She would have been foolish to risk confronting the hospital administrator with such a slender theory. She was impetuous. It was good to have a calmer head on her side. With an effort, she forced it from her mind and got ready for the next interview, with a teacher who wanted to arrange for a tour of the hospital for her fifth-grade students.

Janina was just getting her things together to go home when David walked into the office. Her spirits lifted as if she had just been given a shot of adrenaline. He studied her for a brief moment and then leaned an elbow against the door frame.

"You won't believe this. I just heard over the radio that Judge Thorpe reversed his decision. They're going to begin aerial spraying of the town by tomorrow night."

Janina swore. "Dear God. If what we believe is true—that the malathion is proving to be lethal—they could be putting the whole town in jeopardy."

David nodded. "No question about it...that's *if* the malathion is really unsafe." He wiped his hand across his mouth. "But darn it, Janina. Much as it has been used over a period of years, it's hard for me to believe it's dangerous."

She shook her head. "Don't let me down now, David. If we wait until we have absolute proof, it could be too late. I don't know if I can do this alone, but I will if I have to."

He saw the tears glisten in her eyes and he held out his arms. Janina hesitated only a minute, then walked toward him and put her arms around his waist. David had a talent for comforting her when she needed it most.

She remembered a night nearly four years ago when she had been working the three-to-eleven shift in ICU. One of her patients, a young musician who had been in an auto accident, had suddenly turned sour and before she or anyone could get him up to OR, he had expired. Carl, his name was. He was a sweet, sensitive young man who was about to marry his publicity person. Janina had cried for him and his fiancée, cried more than a nurse should have. But David had understood, and when he took her home that night, he held her in his arms and whispered all the wonderfully endearing things she wanted to hear.

And now he brought the warmth of his arms to her again, but she was older now and usually managed to control her emotions.

Even the warmth of David's arms couldn't forestall the chill that permeated Janina's body. "I don't understand," she murmured against his shoulder. "Why would the judge reverse his decision?"

"My guess is that it had to be some pretty powerful pressure from above. That's the only answer."

"But from whom? Not the fruit growers. They have a strong coalition, but it's not strong enough to influence a judge." She moved away from him. "I can't just stand here. I've got to do something, David. I'm going upstairs to talk to the administrator."

"I'll go with you."

"No. You can't afford to jeopardize your medical career. You'd better wait in my office."

"I'm going with you, Janina."

She nodded, and mentally gave him a gold star.

Randolph Baker's cordiality evaporated like fog in the noonday sun when he discovered the reason for their visit.

"Janina, my dear," he said as he patted her shoulder. "Don't we keep you busy enough downstairs in your little office? Why do you have to go around digging up skeletons where there aren't any? I heard about the ruckus you created at the staff meeting the other day." He reminded Janina of a white-haired congressman, and she cautioned herself to be diplomatic.

"Mr. Baker, I appreciate your position. I do realize

you are powerless to go to the authorities without proof
of the connection between the spray program and the
incidence of acute pancreatitis. But now I'm confident
we have that proof.''

David pulled out a map of the city and spread it over
the huge antique mahogany desk that was centered in
the spacious, beautifully appointed office.

Janina flipped open her notebook. ''I have here a
list of the addresses of the patients involved.'' She
gestured to the map. ''We've highlighted the locations
here and, as you see, they are all centered around an
area in the foothills. To date, that's where the county
has concentrated the malathion spray.''

''Janina, Janina.'' Randolph Baker shook his head
as he attempted to soothe her.

She took a deep breath and counted to ten. ''You're
not a medical man, Mr. Baker, but surely your staff
has impressed upon you the fact that having so many
cases of pancreatitis all of a sudden is just too unusual
to be considered a coincidence.''

''Now, now, young lady. Dr. Madison here will
doubtless agree that pancreatitis is common among
alcoholics.'' He laughed. ''And we certainly have our
share of them here in the valley. . . what with the high-
technology industry and all.''

Janina didn't want David involved. She interrupted
before he could speak. ''There's no connection
betw—''

Randolph Baker was losing his cool. His face had
begun to flush above his snow-white button-down collar, and he took a seat behind his desk. ''Young lady.
You are nothing more than a glorified nurse turned office clerk. You are in no way qualified to make a judgment. Now sit down and be quiet.''

She wasn't about to sit down, but she waited as he appeared to mull over thoughts in his head, then spoke. "I rather thought you might continue to dig into this, so I did a little detective work on my own. It seems the Department of Agriculture has been faced with the fruit fly in many parts of the country. This isn't the first time they've begun a massive spray campaign." He shoved some photocopies in front of her.

"Here are some statistics having to do with the past use of malathion as an insecticide. I think you should study them carefully and then reconsider before you go around trying to stir up trouble. And in the future, my dear—" his voice softened "—kindly confine your work to your office. We have doctors to take care of the medical questions at Mercy Hospital." He stood up. "Now, if you'll excuse me, I have another appointment. So nice to meet you, Dr. Madison. I've heard good things about your work when you were on the staff here at Mercy."

"Mr. Baker. You've got to—" Janina began, but David put his hand on her arm and spoke quietly.

"Come on. Let's go."

"No! I have to—"

"Wise advice, Dr. Madison. Miss Scott seems a bit overwrought."

Janina spun around and left the office without looking back. Once the door closed behind them, she turned to David. "If I weren't a lady, I'd tell that . . . that egotistical jerk what I think of him."

"It wouldn't help. After all, who are you but a plain, glorified nurse turned office clerk?"

She drew a strangled breath. "Why you—" and then she saw his face and realized that he was only trying to defuse her temper. She grumbled. "If I had stayed in there a minute longer, I would have punctured the old windbag.''

"Why do you think I went with you? I know what hospital administrators can be like. They answer to a higher god than we common people do. I also know the limits of your low boiling point when you are convinced you're right.''

"I suppose I should thank you, but I'm too darn mad. I'm going home before something else happens.''

"Good. You need a rest.''

"Rest? Don't be ridiculous. I'm going to map out some new strategy.''

"Want some help?''

"You mean you're still interested?'' She looked at him in wonderment.

"Listen, my wide-eyed angel of mercy. If I were any more interested, you'd call the cops.''

She darted her tongue over her lips. "Are we talking about the same thing?''

He put his arm around her waist and walked her down the thickly carpeted corridor to the staff elevator. "You interpret it your way and I'll take mine.''

They stopped at a restaurant for an early dinner, then David took her home and they sat talking in the den. David leaned back in his favorite lounger and linked his hands behind his head. "I don't know, Janina. If these reports on malathion are true, I don't see how it could be the culprit.''

"But it has to be. What else is there?''

"I wish I knew. Maybe—'' He was interrupted by a bell tinkling in the kitchen. "What the devil is that?''

"That's Cinnamon coming home from her evening tour of the neighborhood.''

"She rings the bell? Can't she just howl like other cats?"

Janina laughed. "She's automated. I used to date a fellow who was a technician for Langtree Labs. He wired the door so that if Cinn wants to go out or in, all she has to do is push a button. It rings a bell and opens and closes her cat door. That way, no other cats can sneak in."

"Clever." David sounded bored.

"You haven't heard the rest. He also rigged a buzzer to go off at a certain time. When it does, Cinnamon hops up on the shelf and pushes the button. It trips a lever that spills premeasured food into the fish tank. Gary thought she needed to earn her keep."

"And just how did dear old Gary make *you* earn your keep?"

Janina shook her head. "Not nice, David. Would you believe me if I told you I cooked dinner for him?"

"Then I take it he's not around anymore."

"You cut right to the quick, don't you?"

He looked over at her. "Well? Do you still see him?"

"No. He moved up to Seattle to work at a branch office of Langtree Labs."

He breathed a sigh of relief. "That ought to keep him at a safe distance. Langtree Labs must have done all right during the recession. I see their name all over town. I can't believe how much they've grown since I was here three years ago."

"You probably haven't seen the half of it. Langtree has bought up so many businesses and small industries in Willowbrook that they practically own the town. They've even bought into the New Orleans insurance foundation that runs the hospital."

"I thought there must be some fresh money there, what with the new wing going up."

"Um. It's going to be the new outpatient clinic. The old clinic will be turned over to the lab for expansion into research."

"Nice. That does take money."

"They seem to have it. Unfortunately, not much of it sifts down to the hospital employees."

"Aren't you happy working here?"

"I'm not really unhappy. I think I might be ready for a change of scene, though." She got up and turned on another table lamp. "Speaking of change of scene. I decided I am going up to visit my parents tomorrow."

"Oh." He wondered if he were partly to blame for her wanting to get away. Had he pushed a little too hard? Had he taken it too much for granted that she still loved him? He tightened his jaw and Janina saw the muscle twitch in his cheek.

"I need to talk to Debbie." Janina wondered why she found it necessary to explain to him, but the expression on his face was so vulnerable that she suddenly felt protective.

He stood and began buttoning his brown sports coat. "I guess I'd better go back to my motel and let you get some rest."

He obviously was waiting for Janina to demur, but she kept silent, so David made ready to leave. "Be sure to give my best to your family." He took her hand. "Come on. Walk out to the car with me."

His hand was pleasantly warm. Disturbingly so, Janina thought. A part of her wanted him to stay with her. Perceptive as he was, she became afraid that he was aware of it when his thumb began tracing erotic

circles on the back of her hand. Was he deliberately trying to arouse her or was it simply one of the small, intimate gestures that came so naturally to David? She
reminded herself that he was only here for a short time.
Getting involved could be fatal.

Considering it was Friday, the complex was quiet.
Maybe this was a Reno weekend. Some of the younger
residents had gotten in the habit of chartering a bus and
driving up to Reno or Lake Tahoe to spend the weekend
attending shows and gambling. The thought of it bored
her.

As they walked across to the visitors' parking lot, a
low droning sound stopped them and they listened intently. "What the devil is that?" David asked.

"Damn. It's the helicopter squadron. They've started the aerial spray program."

"I can't see them."

"You will. They fly at rooftop level in groups of
four. I don't like it. There's something evil about the
way they hover just on the edge of darkness."

"How come they spray at night?"

"Fewer people are around then. Malathion may not
be harmful, but they sure don't recommend that people
stand out under the spray."

They had reached the Mercedes. She put her hand on
the car door as he got in. "If you don't want the paint
job ruined on this bucket of bolts, you'd better head for
your motel and its covered parking lot."

He put his hand over hers. "Drive carefully tomorrow, Janina. You staying overnight?"

"I don't know. Probably. It depends on how everything is."

He picked up her hand and lifted her fingertips to his
mouth. His lips were warm and inviting. She drew away.

"I . . . I think I'd better go in before the helicopters come. They may start spraying this area, too."

"I'll miss you, Janina."

"Good night, David." She turned and ran toward the house, then stopped under the overhang of her front porch to watch David drive away.

Overhead the helicopters were coming closer. The sound resembled the beating wings of so many pre-historic monsters risen from some primeval swamp in search of prey. The noise was frightening enough, but as the helicopters approached, she saw their dark shapes silhouetted against the sliver of moon. On each craft there was a single searchlight, the eye of the Cyclops, moving in slow circles as if it savored the hunt.

Chapter Four

Janina flattened herself against the wall of the building, fear and fascination warring with her emotions. The grounds of the condominium complex were deserted. It occurred to Janina that anyone with any sense at all would take shelter indoors. Yet something drew her to witness the flight of the spray planes as they carved a low path just barely above the cedar shake rooftops.

The vibration from the helicopter engines beat against her chest. Or was it her own heartbeat? And then she noticed the smell. Surprisingly, it left a taste in her mouth...like licorice; sweet, sickeningly so. Like the smell of death.

Janina wished fervently that David had stayed with her. But that was stupid. She mustn't become dependent on him. It had taken her a long time to stop leaning. Now she was on her own and it felt good...most of the time.

Her breath returned gradually as the helicopters passed overhead, their sound slowly diminishing like the flutter of dying moths near a flame. She wondered at her fear, now that they were gone. Once again the night took on its California magic and she sighed as she opened the door and went inside.

JANINA DELAYED HER DEPARTURE the next morning in the hope that David might call, but by ten-thirty she still hadn't heard from him and could wait no longer. The drive up 280 and across the San Mateo Bridge to Route 17 was always a pleasure. Even now in the midst of summer when the foothills were golden-brown, it was the most beautiful freeway in the country. In the distance, toward Redwood City, Belmont and San Francisco, she saw banks of clouds rolling in over the tops of the mountains. It was cooling off rapidly. She opened the window and let the breeze drift in from the salt flats across the bay.

As she approached the county line, a police officer directed her into a single lane of traffic that ran bumper to bumper for a short distance. When it was her turn, they asked her if she had any fresh fruit with her and she told them no and was allowed to continue on her way. It was a simple procedure, but it reminded her of the hospital and of David, and it was a relief to arrive finally at her parents' comfortable colonial-style home on Meadowlark Lane in Castro Valley, where Janina had grown up.

It was obvious that Debbie and her mother had gotten into another argument just before Janina arrived. Her mother hugged her, but briefly. A sure sign that she was tense and on the verge of declaring an all-out war on her youngest daughter.

Janina felt a pang of guilt. Her mother had a tendency to be fragile despite her outward appearance of strength. She looked good for her age. Both her father and mother kept active, and except for the streaks of gray in her hair, one would have thought she was much younger. But beneath the healthy glow was a history of illness.

She really wasn't up to coping with Debbie, who at

seventeen was enough to try anyone's patience. Janina had more success controlling her younger sister than anyone, but the time between her visits had gotten longer and her influence had begun to diminish.

Debbie, dressed in skintight jeans and a T-shirt that exaggerated her generous bustline, was sprawled in the family room when Janina and her mother walked in. Debbie jumped up and hugged Janina exuberantly. "Am I ever glad you're here. Maybe you can talk some sense into Mom's head. She treats me like I'm still fifteen."

"Well, you certainly act like it sometimes," their mother said as she picked up the duster she had been using on the corner shelves.

Janina cringed. She hated fights. She had gone through her own teenage crisis, but it seemed like eons ago. Janina, at Debbie's age, had known exactly what she wanted in life and how to go about getting it. Or so she thought. It had made the transition from childhood to adulthood less traumatic. Debbie's problem was that she had no set goals.

The argument was heating up. Her mother's face was pink from her increased blood pressure. Oddly, it made her look younger in spite of the way it emphasized the tiny new lines in her face.

Debbie's eyes were dark with anger and she had begun to twist a strand of her long brown hair into a sleek coil. Janina had learned to duck under those conditions, but now she interrupted the argument.

"Listen, you guys. I'd love to go for a walk. My legs are stiff from riding in the car. Want to come along, Deb?"

She looked sullen. "Stiff, after an hour's drive? You really are getting old, Jan." She pulled herself out of the chair and pushed down the legs of her jeans. "Sure, why not? I could use some fresh air."

"You be back pretty soon, you two. Your father will be home for lunch and I don't want to keep him waiting." Her mother gave Janina a bigger hug. "I really am glad to have you home, Janina. It seems like ages since you were here."

Janina smiled. It had been less than a month, but her mother always said the same thing whether it was two days or two months.

The neighborhood had changed quite a bit since the days when she attended junior high and high school. Groups of town houses had sprung up where once there were orchards. It was an affluent section of town, with well-kept houses and grounds, a tennis and a swim club. The church that the family attended was within walking distance. Janina had sung in the church choir all during her school years. Down two blocks and around the corner was where Ricky Johnson, her first boyfriend, used to live. She wondered if he still chewed gum when he kissed.

Debbie had begun to relax the minute they turned the corner. "God. I don't know how much more of that I can take. How did you survive it, anyway?"

"It wasn't so bad once I realized why they were concerned. Besides, I left home right after high school to go into nurse's training. Haven't you come to a decision about what you want to do?"

"Nah. Mom keeps after me to get a job, but I can't find anything except waitressing. I'd rather die than do that. I can't stand the smell of food cooking."

"Have you ever thought about nursing?"

Debbie flipped her dark hair over her shoulder. "I couldn't handle the screaming kids. I remember how it was the time I visited you when you were working in Pediatrics. It sounded like feeding time at the zoo.''

"You could specialize in geriatrics. You do so well with older people.''

"Except for Mom.''

"She's worried about you.'' Janina undid the knot on her turquoise silk scarf and pulled it from around her neck. "I hear you've been going around with the Johnny Espinosa crowd. That's rough company, Deb. What ever happened to you and Doug Fairfax? When I saw him last week, he asked all about you. I thought you were nuts about him.''

Perspiration vied for space among the few tiny freckles on Debbie's nose. "Doug doesn't have time for me since he started premed. He's always at school or working at the convalescent home in Willowbrook. I never get to see him.''

"Too bad. He's a terrific guy.''

"I know. I used to like him a lot.''

"I have the feeling you still do.'' Debbie didn't affirm or deny it, and Janina was sure she had hit on the truth. "Debbie. Would it do any good if I asked you to go easy on the drinking? It cannot only easily become a habit but it does awful things to your insides, not to mention what it does to your skin.''

Debbie gave her a look. "Now tell me that you never drink.''

"Truthfully, I rarely do. But there's a difference between taking a drink and being a drinker.'' Janina put her arm around her sister's shoulder. "Listen, Deb. We love you and we care about what happens to you. You have to live your own life; I'm the first one to admit that. But I just don't want you to get started in the wrong direction. Sometimes it's hard to find your way back. Okay?''

Debbie shrugged. "I can take care of myself. You don't have to worry about me. Johnny's not that bad. Besides, he's cute and he has a new set of wheels. Doug drives his dad's van when we go out. Can you believe that? It's always half full of air-conditioning equipment."

"Sure, but you have to think ahead. Doug is ambitious. He's trying hard to make something of himself in spite of his poor background. How does that compare to Johnny Espinosa's future?"

Debbie didn't answer, but Janina knew she had given her something to think about. It was the best she was able to manage that weekend. At any rate, the air was cleared for the rest of the day and when their father got home, everyone was in good spirits.

Janina spent the night in her old room, which still bore reminders of her student days. The dresser drawer held her nurse's cap, carefully wrapped in clear plastic. Seeing it, she felt an overwhelming urge to return to active nursing. Maybe someday she'd take a course in preventative medicine. She lay back on the bed and studied the plaster whorls that bordered the ceiling. Maybe in an outpatient clinic she would finally be able to do the kind of nursing she wanted to; helping people stay well. She squinted her eyes and imagined herself back in school. It was strange coming home again. She felt far removed from the problems at the hospital, and even further away from David.

That was part of the trouble. Although she had fought against it, she missed him and was glad to get back to her own condominium. She had gone to church and had lunch with the family, then made it back to Willowbrook by two in the afternoon.

It occurred to her that she kept watching for a certain

dark burgundy Mercedes to drive into the visitors' parking space, but by five-thirty she had given up. By seven that evening she was beginning to feel the dull edge of depression hanging over her like a rusty guillotine blade.

If David had gone back to San Diego, she certainly couldn't blame him. But damn, he could have at least said goodbye. It would have been better if he had never come back at all. In just two days he had managed to upset her life completely.

David could be perfectly irritating at times. True, he was even exasperating sometimes, but he was also generous with his time, confident enough in himself to allow her to be right once in a while, was warm and loving and had a good sense of humor...and he could cook! If she had been keeping score, she would have known long ago that no other man she had met could quite measure up to David. But he had caused her so much pain. She mustn't forget that, ever.

Cinnamon didn't help matters. She kept wandering around the house, searching the rooms and corners. When she couldn't find David, she perched on his chair, swinging her tail and grumbling in a dark brown funk.

"You might as well cheer up, Toots," Janina said, scratching the cat's chin. "David isn't coming and you'd better get used to it." She went into the kitchen and started heating a can of split pea soup. Going into the den, she switched on the tape deck and after fighting a losing battle with her better judgment, slipped in the Mantovani cassette that had been David's favorite. At that moment the doorbell rang. It was David.

Fortunately, Cinnamon pushed her way in front of Janina and got to David first. Janina was glad. It gave her a chance to restrain herself. Otherwise she might have thrown herself into his arms like an utter fool.

"David." She gave him a noncommittal hug, sandwiching the cat in the middle. "It's nice to see you." *Talk about an understatement,* she thought. It was a good thing he couldn't read her mind.

He put the cat back down on the floor and kissed Janina's cheek in a distracted, casual way. Janina had expected a little more than Cinnamon had gotten, but David seemed preoccupied. "When did you get back?" he asked.

"Not long ago," she lied, not wanting him to know that she had returned early in the hope he would be waiting for her.

"How are your folks?"

"About the same. Debbie's having a rough time growing up. She said to tell you hi."

"And your parents? Are they ready to draw and quarter me?" He made a joke of it, but he cared more than he let her know. The weekend was endless while she was away. He couldn't begin to think of an entire life without her.

Janina smiled. "I think my folks would like to see you. Mother would, anyway, but then you always were able to manage her. Dad will come around eventually."

"Eventually? That sounds like we might have some kind of future."

She was surprised by the naked hope shining in his eyes, but she wasn't secure enough to encourage him. "San Diego might as well be at the ends of the earth. Long-distance relationships don't work very well, David."

"It doesn't have to be long distance. San Diego is a nice place to live, the hospital is a great place to work."

"Have you set up a practice in addition to being on the staff of the hospital?"

He hesitated. "A small practice. Susan required a

great deal of my time. I plan to use some of her money to set up an outpatient clinic for the less privileged.''

"But that's wonderful. Will you stay on at the hospital?"

"Probably. At the moment most of my plans are in limbo...until I find out...''

He looked distracted again and turned his head in the direction of the kitchen. "What the devil is that awful smell?"

"Oh, God. The soup. It's boiling over."

Normally David would have teased her about not being able to boil water, but he refrained. It wasn't at all like him. Janina stole a glance at him while she cleaned up the scorched mess.

"What's up, David? You look perturbed."

"You seem so relaxed and cheerful since you got back that I've been trying to decide whether or not to tell you."

She studied his face. If he only knew how depressed she had been before he arrived, he would be amazed. Aloud she said, "Tell me what? You know you can't keep anything from me."

"I just heard that the fourth case brought into City Medical is another resident of the foothill section. So all of the cases that seem out of the ordinary have developed within a mile and a half of one another."

Janina threw the cruddy sponge into the sink and swore softly. "And that's a development that is semi-rural. Half-acre to acre plots. Countless home orchards, and it's also where the county has been concentrating the malathion spray. Now tell me it's a coincidence."

"It isn't impossible."

"Dammit, David, you don't believe that any more than I do."

"You're right. I don't. And I agree that we have to do something about it."

He motioned to the scorched pan of soup. "Your dinner, I take it?"

"Not anymore. I couldn't care less. I ate lunch at my mother's and I'm still stuffed. You know how she cooks."

He grinned. "Yeah, terrific."

"As long as you don't object to eight kinds of starches topped with gravy and homemade apple pie à la mode."

"The great American custom. I ate a sandwich an hour ago and I'm not hungry."

She put the pan in the sink and filled it with water. "I have an idea. Want to go for a ride?"

David looked puzzled. "Sure, but what's that supposed to accomplish?"

"I want to go out to the foothills and drive around. You know what's sitting right in the middle of all those orchards?" She didn't wait for him to answer. "It's Langtree Labs. I was out there a few times a couple of years ago with a guy I knew."

"Yeah. I remember you telling me about the electronics genius who automated your cat."

Janina gave him a look. "They make pharmaceutical supplies: vitamins, aspirin, that kind of stuff."

"So what's the connection?"

She shrugged. "Nothing, probably, unless maybe they manufacture the malathion there. I'd like to look around and see if we can spot any tank trucks, and look over the area where the helicopters spray."

"I really think you're wasting your time. Besides, it's

going to be dark soon.'' He saw the disappointment in her face and relented. ''Okay, Jan. If you really want to go, I'll go with you.''

''Good. Your car or mine?''

''You've got to be kidding.''

JANINA LEANED BACK against the pearl-gray velvet upholstery and rested her head. ''It's not bad, but considering the price, I thought a Mercedes would be roomier.''

''I'll bet you'd say the same thing about a Lotus.''

She grinned. ''I'm cursed with long legs.''

He looked down at the way her jeans stretched across her thighs. ''Some curse. Most women would give a few million to have legs like that.''

Janina was left speechless by the compliment. She wanted to believe that David never said anything he didn't mean. The glow that began in the pit of her stomach made up for her earlier depression. She was glad she had worn her pale gold silk blouse. David liked the color and it brought out the burnished highlights in her hair. It wasn't smart, dressing to please David, but she had been powerless to stop herself.

It seemed so right sitting next to him that it was hard to remind herself that three years had gone by. Three years he had spent living with another woman. Maybe he had done the moral thing in looking after Susan until her death, but it didn't make it easier to know that Susan had come first while Janina had died her own private death in rejection.

David broke into her thoughts. ''We must be within the main spray area now. We just crossed Fullerton Street.''

Janina straightened. It had been a few months since

she had been out this way. Several new buildings had gone up, all neatly landscaped and looking as if they had been there for five years. She saw a street sign and managed to get her bearings. "If you grab a left at Vernal, then right on Arpeggio, it should lead you right up to the parking lot of Langtree Labs. I can't think of anything else nearby except for the series of housing tracts."

"I'll drive up to the lab and turn around."

As they approached, Janina leaned forward. "That's strange. They've put up a fence. It used to be wide open."

"And there's a guard gate, too," David said, easing up on the accelerator.

"I can't believe it. I've been here a half-dozen times and I drove right up to the front entrance and walked in. There wasn't even a fence around it then. Now it looks like they have a chain-link fence around the whole perimeter, at least as far as I can see."

David's face tightened. "Let's find out what the story is." He swung the car into the drive and pulled to a stop when the guard came out of his station and held up his hand.

"Good evening. State the nature of your business, sir, if you please."

"Certainly. I'm Dr. Madison. Do you need some ID?"

"Yes, sir, and we'll need to see your pass and one for the lady."

David rummaged in his pockets. "I think I must have left them at home. My wife and I are here at the request of William Langtree."

"Oh, I'm sorry, sir, I didn't realize. If you'll excuse me a moment, I'll just call to let him know you've arrived. Wait here, please."

They had little choice but to stay since he was careful to keep the gate secured. Janina looked over at David, who remained impassive. Her palms had begun to sweat, and she was certain anyone within a half-block could hear her heart pounding against her ribs.

"David, what are you going to do when they let us in?"

"We'll think of something. Keep quiet. Here he comes."

The guard's face was like stone. "Thank you for waiting so patiently. May I see your driver's license, please?"

David handed it over. The guard studied it for a moment. Janina was shaking inside. There was something odd going on here, something dreadfully wrong. She was beginning to get scared.

The guard returned the license to David, then dropped his hands to his hips. Was it a coincidence that his gun holster was just inches below his belt? Janina held her breath as the guard stepped back from the car.

"I'm sorry, Dr. Madison. Mr. William Langtree is not in at the present. His secretary has no record of an appointment for you and Mrs. Madison. I wonder if the two of you would just step into the building for a minute? Mr. Langtree's assistant would like to make his apology in person."

"Thank you, but an apology isn't necessary. We'll come back another time."

The guard narrowed his gaze. "It will take only a minute. Just park your car right here next to the booth." He stepped back to allow David to back up.

The car was already running. David shoved it into gear and told the guard that he must have misunderstood where Bill planned to meet them. Spinning the car in a tight circle, David sped away from the gate, back toward the main street.

Janina slowly let out her breath. "My God! What was that all about?"

"That is what's known as extreme security precautions. I strongly suspect we were about to undergo intensive questioning about why we were there."

Janina studied David's face. "How did you just happen to know there's a William Langtree?"

"I didn't, but Langtree is a family dynasty. Every self-respecting dynasty names at least one son William. It was just dumb luck."

"I don't feel very lucky."

He laughed dryly. "You would have felt less lucky if the Langtree Mafia had gotten a chance to question us." He swung the car sharply around the next corner. "Let's see what's on the other side of this place."

Although they drove as close as they could, any roads that came within several hundred yards of the buildings had been blocked off and the fence had been electrified. It was fast growing dark.

David, driving slowly so they could see, suddenly pulled off the road, into a grove of trees. Moments later a security truck cruised by. David sat there for a few minutes with the motor running.

"You think he's looking for us?" Janina asked.

"I doubt it. I just don't like someone following me."

"I'd sure like to get a better look at this place, but it looks as if this is as close as we can get." She held her hand up for silence. "Listen, it's the helicopters. They're going to start spraying. W-we'd better get out of here or they'll ruin your car."

David heard the quaver in her voice and patted the seat next to him. She slid over, grateful for the warmth of his hip against hers as he headed the car in the direction of her home.

He looked down at her, so close he could smell the freshness of her hair and the faint lemon rinse he remembered so well. He thought suddenly of the first time they had made love. She had combed her hair up that night in a French twist to go with the black lace gown she had worn to a hospital benefit dance at the club. God, she had looked elegant. There wasn't a man there, young or old, who wouldn't have given anything to have traded places with him that night.

Funny about Janina. One moment, she looked like a kid in her cutoff jeans. The next minute, she was all satin and lace, looking hot and sexy like a pinup in a men's magazine. A woman to match his moods. He liked that. He liked her.

No. If there had ever been a question in his mind, the last few days had erased it. He was in love with Janina. Probably always had been. But things had changed. He wasn't the knight in shining armor that he had once appeared to be to her. Damn! He had a lot to make up for, but he was determined to give it his best shot.

It was quiet for a few minutes as David entered the freeway and merged with the sparse traffic.

Janina looked up at him and met his gaze. "You're worried, too, aren't you?"

"Concerned, yes. Worried, I'm not sure. I guess what I really am is puzzled. There's an answer here somewhere, but we just aren't seeing it."

"There has to be a reason why the cases all center around the spray zone. If it isn't the malathion that's making people sick, what is it? Could they have started using another kind of spray that's more hazardous?"

David nodded. "I've been wondering the same thing.

If they are, is it being manufactured at Langtree Labs? Is that the reason for the heavy security?''

Janina sat up straight. "Oh, David. It makes sense, doesn't it? Why else would they suddenly become so security-conscious? Darn. I wish we could get a better look at that place.''

David glanced in the rearview mirror. "If we don't get out of here, we might get more of a look than we hoped for. I think we're being followed by that same security truck.''

Janina gasped. "I can't believe it. Why would they want to follow us?''

"Move over, Jan, so I can drive, and fasten your seat belt.''

She slid over to give him more room, then pulled the seat belt across her chest and snapped it in place. As the security truck drew up behind them, David swerved suddenly and forced the Mercedes over the low curb that separated the main freeway from the exit. The car shot forward in a burst of speed, barely pausing as it passed a stop sign at the intersection of Valencia Street. It had been too late for the security police to make the exit.

Janina drew a shaky breath. "Do you think we lost them?''

"I don't know. I'll take some back streets, but they'll have my license number and they'll know where to find me.''

"But that's in San Diego." She felt a sudden panic at the thought of him leaving. "You won't be there for weeks. You said you had a month off, didn't you?''

"Yeah. But I wasn't sure I'd be staying here that long.''

"You're not going to leave now, are you, David?''

"That depends a lot on you, Jan." He watched her eyes widen, heard the quick intake of her breath, saw her tongue dart out to moisten her lips. He had gotten to her with that last remark. She still cared about him, whether or not she admitted it, and that small bit of information sent a bubble of warmth singing through his veins.

Janina looked over at his face, but his quick glance told her little except that he was waiting for her to make the decision for him. If he left again, the void would be unendurable. Her hands began to perspire and she furtively rubbed them against the legs of her jeans.

She didn't want him to leave. Her first instinct was to promise anything to get him to stay, but one small door at the back of her mind refused to open and she folded her arms protectively around her.

"I . . . I don't see how you could leave in the middle of all this. So many questions unanswered. I mean, we may have uncovered something that points to whatever or whoever is using chemicals that are responsible for starting an epidemic. You can't just quit in the middle. You have to stay a while longer." She knew it wasn't the answer he had hoped for, but it was safer this way.

David gripped the wheel harder than necessary. *Oh, Janina,* he thought. *Can't you just let go and say it? We need each other. It's our turn now to be together.*

She saw the tightness of his mouth and the way he hunched forward in the seat, both hands holding on to the steering wheel as if it were a lifeline.

"You're awfully quiet, David. Does that mean you want to leave?"

"No. I'll stay, at least until this is settled."

Janina didn't know whether he was referring to the epidemic or to their relationship. The important thing was that he would stay a while longer.

David kept glancing into the rearview mirror, but there was no sign of their pursuers as he eased the car into the parking space at Janina's condo. He was relieved that so far the security police could not connect her with anything. They walked to her door and for a moment both hesitated.

Then Janina looked up at him. "You are coming in, aren't you?"

He grinned. "I thought you'd never ask."

Once inside, Janina was at a loss to know what to do. "Shouldn't we call the police or something?"

"And tell them that we tried to get into the lab under false pretenses and that we thought we were followed? You haven't heard how those things work, I see. It would be us they'd hold for questioning, not the personnel from Langtree Labs."

"But what can we do? Then what do you suggest?"

He blew out his cheeks and braced himself against the kitchen cabinet. "Lord, I don't know."

"If only we could have gotten a closer look at the buildings. I'd like to see them in the daytime, at least from the outside."

"Not much chance of that. It was hard enough at night. It would be impossible in the daytime."

"I guess you're right, but darn it, I feel so helpless."

Later, as they lingered over coffee and avocado, cheese and bacon sandwiches on the patio, David added a layer of alfalfa sprouts to the already-towering stack. "What can you remember from your little trysts with your electronics genius about the way Langtree Labs was laid out?"

Janina gave him a withering look. "It was hardly a tryst. Gary was just showing me around." She leaned back, stretched out her legs beneath the table, and rested her head against the back of the chair. "I can't recall very much about it. The buildings were fewer and not very impressive. There was the main administration building, which connected two wings. The north wing, which was the largest, was devoted to production and distribution. The south wing was experimental. Gary was working there, installing a hermetically sealed, environmentally controlled atmosphere or something. Truthfully, I didn't pay that much attention."

"How could you, with old Gary hanging all over you?"

Janina chuckled. "You sound jealous as a bucktooth, lop-eared teenager." The expression on his face pleased her. Pleased her a little too much, she thought as she sobered. "Why? What difference does it make what the layout is?" Suddenly it struck her. "David! You aren't thinking about sneaking into the lab, are you? My God, you'd be caught for sure. You could go to jail."

"I'd like to say that's what I had in mind, but I wouldn't have the nerve to try to get in there illegally. Besides, I don't know what I could accomplish. I just thought maybe something you recalled seeing might be significant. If you saw big vats of some kind, it could mean they might be producing the new spray on the premises. Or you might have smelled a petroleum-based chemical that could be a clue as to what we're looking for. Most of the aerial sprays have an odor of fuel oil about them."

She shook her head. "I don't remember anything like that. As I remember, the place was clean to the point of being antiseptic. No odors that I can remember . . . except the smell of solder where Gary was connecting a rubber-covered wire cable. I don't know, David. It's so different from what it used to be. So big."

"Um. Well, no point worrying about it now. Come on. I'll help you clear the dishes."

The sudden intimacy of working together in the kitchen bothered Janina and she stopped what she was doing to watch him wipe off the patio table.

"What's up?" he asked as he came back into the kitchen.

"Oh..." She was momentarily embarrassed. "I-I just wondered if you helped Susan in the kitchen, too?"

His face closed in on itself as he thought about his life with Susan. It hadn't been easy, but he didn't regret it. He had done what he had to do to make Susan's last few years less painful. For a moment Janina thought he would ignore the question, but he finally answered.

"For the last two years, Susan wasn't able to get out of her wheelchair. We had a woman come in to cook for us and to do the housework. Before that, Susan did all the cooking. She felt that a man didn't belong in the kitchen."

"But you enjoy it so much," Janina protested.

"I do, given the proper circumstances."

"Which are?"

He looked around him. "A cozy kitchen with shiny wood cabinets and a blue bowl filled with nasturtiums."

She saw the veiled look in his eyes and as he came toward her, she instinctively took a step backward into the corner.

His voice was husky as he closed in on her and braced his hand on the wall behind her shoulder.

"And I like a woman with philodendron curling around her head," he said as he brushed away a vine that lay across her hair.

Chapter Five

Janina looked up at him. "David, no," she pleaded, but somehow it sounded more like yes. When he stroked the back of her neck, she felt the stirring of desire deep in the pit of her stomach. It had been a long time since she had wanted a man, but her body remembered.

He cupped her chin in his hand and lifted her face until it was close to his. His mouth was warm as it brushed against her cheek then traced a path across her forehead to her eyebrow.

She hadn't meant to respond, but she found her lips teasing the tip of his chin, nipping it playfully, testing the barely discernible stubble of beard with her tongue.

He wove his fingers into her hair and cradled her head in his hands, tilting it back until his mouth found hers in a probing, melting kiss.

She wanted it to go on forever. When he finally drew away, his thumbs skimmed across her chin until they found the fullness of her mouth and traced its contour. She trembled and he pulled her against him, the curves of her hip meeting the contoured planes of his muscular body.

They breathed as one; short, ragged breaths that were in themselves an indication of their passion. His hands slid down the length of her back until they came to rest on her hips. Again his mouth found hers in unfulfilled hunger. He moaned as he drew back then pulled her against him and buried his face in her hair.

"Janina, love, I've missed you so much. I've dreamed of holding you like this, feeling your heart pounding against mine."

Janina turned her face against his shirt and held him close. Her body had betrayed her, remembering too well the passion she had known in David's arms. In the span of a moment, she relived the precious hours they had shared together, golden hours she treasured as much as life itself. But she couldn't surrender, not yet. Nor could she manage to back away. It was the buzzer on the fish tank that saved her.

Gary had intended it to be loud enough that Cinnamon could hear it from the patio. She did, and came tearing into the kitchen, whizzed past them and ran into the den.

"What the devil?" David swore as she ran by.

"It's feeding time for the fish." Janina laughed weakly. "Come on into the den and watch."

"Is that your not-too-subtle way of putting me off?"

Janina leaned away from him and placed her hands on his chest. "I'm not denying I want you, David. It wouldn't do any good, anyway. But I can't. Not yet. When it's time—if it ever is—I think we'll both know it."

He studied the way her hair curled about her temples. Her eyes were so sad; bereft. He wanted nothing more than to hold her until the pain went away, but he knew this wasn't the time. Instead, he turned her around to face the hallway.

"All right. Let's go watch old Gary's galley slave at work."

He walked behind her, barely resting his hand on her shoulder. But through the fine gold silk of her blouse, he could still feel the heat of passion waiting to be fulfilled.

Cinnamon had jumped up on the shelf next to the lighted fish tank and was striking the buzzer with her paw. Suddenly it connected and a fine sprinkle of flakes sifted down onto the surface of the water. Black mollies and zebras and tetras converged on the food, completely ignoring the cat who stood transfixed by their shining bodies.

David, standing with his arm around Janina's waist, watched the display. "I can see it now," he murmured. "Ten years from now, it will be Gary's kids who are automated. He'll have them better trained than a family of robots. They'll march single-file to the table, stand at attention until the signal is given to sit, pick up their forks in unison and chew on command." He bent down and nuzzled her hair with his nose. "Keep that in mind when Gary comes back to town looking for you."

Janina leaned her head against David's shoulder. "Gary who?"

He laughed. "Don't try to make up to me now, Jan. I still haven't recovered from my last attempt to seduce you." He looked at his watch. "Maybe I'd better leave before I change my mind."

"What will you do tomorrow?"

"I'm going to rent a typewriter and see if I can get caught up on my correspondence. That is, if I can remember how to use one. I've been using a computer for several years."

"Want to borrow my word processor? I have an extra key to the house." She noticed the intense look in his eyes and she spoke quickly to hide her embarrassment.

"Don't get me wrong, David. I wasn't suggesting you move in. You can work during the daytime while I'm at the hospital."

He laughed. "I was afraid that's what you meant. Do I get kitchen privileges?"

"Of course. I don't have much in the house, so you'll have to pick up what you want at the store."

"The least I can do."

She dug the key out of the desk drawer and handed it to him. "Be careful driving back to your motel. There's always the chance that the security police are still cruising around looking for your car."

He glanced at his watch. "Not likely. It's been nearly four hours."

"It can't be! We just got back about an hour ago."

He grinned. "Time flies when you're having fun." He kissed her lightly on the mouth and left before she had a chance to touch him or even see him to the door.

WORD HAD OBVIOUSLY GOTTEN AROUND THE HOSPITAL that Janina had been upstairs to talk to the administrator and that she had been properly chastised for her transgression. At first some of the staff kept their distance, but as the day progressed they warmed up. Casey, with her usual cavalier attitude, was very vocal.

"Randolph Baker is nothing but an SOB. He's got to be the put-down king of the world. I would've clobbered him."

"I nearly did, but fortunately, David was there and he kept me from digging myself in too deeply. I haven't given up on this. I know there's something going on."

Casey shrugged. "Maybe, but you seem to be the only one who is convinced of it. No one else has said much."

"I think they're afraid. You *know* that things aren't normal, Casey. If I could just get someone in a position of authority to admit it, we'd have a chance of finding out what's causing the sudden increase of pancreatitis. As it is, every time I mention the subject, I feel as if I'm running into a concrete building."

Casey nodded, then abruptly changed the subject. "You mentioned David. David Madison, I presume. You seeing him again?"

Janina sighed. "For the time being. He lives down in San Diego now and it's just a question of time until he goes back."

"What's he doing up here, as if I didn't know?"

"He. . .he has a month's leave from the hospital. His wife died a few months ago, and he's taking some time off to get his life in order."

"Men! God, what we let them do to us. Are you going back to him after the way he walked out on you?"

"But he had a good reason. Susan needed somebody desperately. David was all she had."

"I never thought you'd start defending him, Janina."

"Neither did I, but. . ." She shrugged. "I guess I'm mellowing in my old age."

Casey raised her eyes to the ceiling. "Love heals all wounds, or so they tell me. You are in love with him, aren't you?"

Janina was saved from answering when the alarm buzzer rang for 309 West, Vince Costello's room.

"That's me," Casey said as she took off down the hall. "Come on. It's George Murdock, the post-op pancreatitis."

Janina felt a shiver of dread. She hesitated momentarily, then followed Casey down the hallway and into the patient's room. The first thing she saw was Vince Costello sitting on the edge of the bed, a look of naked fear on his face.

"My god, Scotty, I was just kiddin' him about tyin' on one too many, and he doubled over and started groaning. What the hell did I do?"

Janina quickly pulled the curtains around Vince's bed. "You had nothing to do with it, Vince. I told you that Mr. Murdock is recovering from surgery. He's been very ill and recovery isn't always as rapid as we'd like. You mustn't blame yourself. We're just grateful that you were sharp enough to think of hitting the emergency call button in the bathroom. It brought his nurse in a hurry."

Vince looked a little relieved, but Janina was still concerned about his flushed face. She smiled, hoping to relax him. "If you'll let me hold your hand for a minute, I'd like to check your pulse."

He managed a grin. "For you, Scotty, anything."

"Good. Well, you seem to be your own sexy self. I think I'd better get out of here while I still have my reputation intact. We'll just leave the curtain drawn for a few minutes while they're taking care of Mr. Murdock. I'll check back with you later, Vince."

Casey had her hands full. She looked up at Janina and nodded her thanks. They were preparing to move the patient, bed and all, and it took a few precious minutes to unhook suction and the other support equipment. Janina noted symptoms of internal bleeding. She looked up at Casey who nodded.

"Hemorrhagic. They're setting up for him in OR. Get the locks, will you?"

Janina ran to the foot of the bed and snapped up the locks that kept the bed from rolling. Casey and the two nursing assistants had it in motion seconds later as Janina went ahead to clear the way to the OR elevator.

Once the patient was turned over to the OR team, Casey and Janina walked back toward the elevator.

Janina was angry and frightened at the same time. "We're going to lose him, aren't we?"

"Could be. He's hemorrhagic now and he's already tested out positive on seven of the twelve Adverse Prognostic Signs. If he survives surgery, we've got a chance, but..." She spread her hands. "Listen, I'll catch you later. I've got to get back to the floor. Thanks for doing your thing with Vince. You sure calmed him down, but I'm not surprised. He's crazy about you."

Janina shrugged. "He's crazy about anything in a skirt."

After she left Casey, Janina stopped in at Physical Therapy to check on Nurse O'Connor. Things were reasonably quiet. She was assisting a tough-looking football player up a set of wooden steps. His face was bathed in perspiration and he gritted his teeth as he lifted first one foot and then the other.

Janina watched them for a few minutes. O'Connor was firm in giving her instructions but not to the point of being cruel.

As O'Connor reached up to adjust his balance, she grimaced in pain and the color drained from her face.

Janina quickly stepped forward. "What is it, Mrs. O'Connor? Are you all right?"

The nurse whirled around in shock. "Of course I'm all right. Excuse me. I'm very busy."

"I'm sorry. I didn't mean to interrupt. I'd like to talk to you when you have a minute."

There was no response and Janina left. On the way to her office she thought about the explosion of pain that had washed over O'Connor's face. Was it possible that the pain accounted for her extremely bad attitude toward patients? She mentally reviewed O'Connor's profile. A single parent of three. Her husband walked out on her seven years ago. Mother in a nursing home. Could it be that she was afraid of losing her job if she admitted she was ill? Her responsibilities for her family would certainly be a contributing factor. Janina made a mental note to look into the situation.

Upon returning to her office, Janina discovered that she had two appointments to take care of before she could go home for the evening. One ambulatory patient wanted help in filling out disability forms for the state, the other appointment was with the family of a patient who wanted to arrange for someone from the visiting nurses' association to call on them after the patient was released from the hospital.

Tedious jobs, both of them. Not normally, though, Janina admitted. But anything would seem tedious when she was so eager to go home. Would David still be there? She shoved her papers into the desk and locked the drawer with uncommon haste. *This is silly,* she told herself. But it didn't slow her down for a minute.

As she drove across town, she wondered what her feelings really were for David. He stirred a wanton desire in her that had lain dormant for a long, long time. Being with him made her feel younger and more female, more completely alive. She recognized the fact that David was the only person she could speak frankly with about her suspicions and concern over the pancreatitis enigma. She was comfortable with him, relaxed. The need for him went far deeper than that, but she couldn't afford the luxury of putting a name to her feelings.

It took forever to unlock the front door. When she

did, disappointment hit her in the face like a wet dish-cloth. The house was quiet, empty. The normal, every-day sounds of the fish tank bubbler and the clock over the stereo, seemed to emphasize the loneliness. David had already gone back to his motel.

"Damn!" she whispered aloud.

Cinnamon strutted into the kitchen, took one sniff of her food and backed away, shaking one front paw and then the other. Janina gave her a playful cuff on the backside. "Don't be so fussy. Eat your food and stop complaining."

Cinnamon looked reproachful, but she rubbed her head against Janina's leg as a last-minute gesture of peace. Janina picked her up and walked over to the refrigerator. It was then that she found the note from David.

Janina. We're going horseback riding, okay? I fixed sandwiches and a thermos of coffee. Went to the store to get some fruit. Be ready when I get back so we can go before dark if it sounds in-teresting.

"Oh, David." She shook her head in wonderment as she folded the note and held it against her cheek. "How well you know me. Oh, no, what am I going to wear?"

Cinnamon slanted her ears back against her head and ran toward her cat door as Janina bounded toward the bedroom to search through the clothes in her closet.

She had hardly gotten out of her dress before the front door opened and she heard David call.

"Hi, Janina. It's me. Where are you?" He was com-ing down the hall.

She nearly panicked as she grabbed something to

cover her near-nakedness. The door was too far away for her to close it in time.

"I—I'm in here, David. I'll be ready in a minute."

He was at the doorway then and he looked in. A pulse began to pound in David's throat as he saw the whiteness of her breasts in stark relief against her suntanned skin. Suddenly it was as if all the fantasies he had concocted during the past year were here, almost within reach. He longed to go to her and hold her and caress her until her eyes burned with the passion he had once kindled. He knew instinctively that she wouldn't fight him. Given a few minutes alone with her in her bedroom, he could weaken her resistance. But he didn't want it that way. This time, this time he had to wait until she was ready.

For an agonizing moment, his eyes widened and Janina thought he might come in, but he reached for the doorknob and closed the door.

"Sorry," he said, and there was a ragged edge to his voice as the door clicked shut. "I forgot you had to change clothes."

Neither of them mentioned the incident later, when Janina went into the kitchen dressed in jeans and red-checkered cotton blouse and boots. David looked trim and sporty in jeans and a blue plaid shirt with a flap neckline that was left unbuttoned. It reminded Janina of the way he looked on their first day together at the beach.

"We'd better be off if we want to get in our ride before the stables close," he said.

"Where are we going?"

"Foothill Ranch Stables."

Janina stopped. "But that's out toward the Langtree Labs, isn't it?"

He nodded as he kissed her briefly. "So it is. You ready?"

FOOTHILL RANCH STABLES HAD DEFINITELY SEEN better days, Janina thought. The pastureland had been grazed down to the roots and the horses were a rheumy lot, standing around in the shade of a decrepit live oak tree that had most of the bark rubbed off the trunk.

David slung the soft-sided picnic basket over the back of a sleepy-eyed bay gelding whose only claim to life was a tail that twitched at a nonexistent fly. "I don't think we're going to break any speed records with these two. They look like fugitives from a glue factory."

Janina patted the flanks of her strawberry roan who swung her head back apprehensively. "Watch your language, David. I think this one is not as dumb as she looks." She mounted, then waited for David as she studied the directions they could take.

It occurred to her that they might be able to get a closer look at the Langtree Laboratory grounds, but after the negative reactions she had experienced all day at the hospital, she was almost afraid to suggest it.

Instead she asked, "Is there a park out here where we can have our picnic?"

He looked at her in mock horror. "Where's your pioneer spirit? All we need is a grassy spot. I borrowed your old beach blanket from the closet in the patio." Reining in his horse, he nudged it in the ribs with his knee. "I remember a shady grove of trees a mile or two to the south. Why don't we give it a try?"

It was in the direction of the Langtree Labs property. Janina shot a look at David, but he was apparently oblivious of her interest. He was in one of those confusing, uncommunicative moods where he seemed to be enjoying some secret excitement.

It crossed her mind that maybe he was planning to try to seduce her. She wouldn't put it past him. He was the original nature boy. More than once they had let their lovemaking get out of hand in the seductive solitude of a woodsy glen or on the deck of a borrowed cabin cruiser drifting a mile or so off the Santa Cruz coast.

David finally returned her look, his face choir-boy innocent, guileless. "Something wrong?"

She shook her head. "Not yet, anyway."

The horses came together on the narrow tree-edged path that bordered the road. David's knee nudged Janina's. The contact triggered warm sensations all along Janina's spine. Was it an accident? He appeared not to notice. That made it worse. She hated to think the chemistry was all one-sided. A slight touch of the reins on the horse's flanks moved her in front of David's horse.

It was a quiet, bucolic neighborhood with small ranch-style homes set at random along the opposite side of the road. Only one person was in sight—a man watering some apricot trees that were part of a fruit orchard bordering the front of his property. Janina recognized him.

As they approached his house, she waved and headed the horse across the road to greet him.

"Mr. Gartner? I'm Janina Scott. We met at the hospital when I helped you fill out the forms for your wife's Medicare."

He shaded his eyes against the glare, and Janina marveled again that one face could hold so many wrinkles. "Sure. I remember you now, but you looked different at first."

"This is my friend, Dr. Madison."

"You one of them who's taking care of my Martha's pancreas?"

David shook his head. " 'Fraid not. I'm just visiting up here from San Diego."

"My Martha's okay, isn't she, Miss Scott?"

"I saw her this morning and she is doing very well."

"They tried to tell me she was an alcoholic. Sure pissed me off." He looked apologetic then went on. "It don't seem fair that she got sick. My Martha's healthy as a horse. Now me, I've been in the hospital a half-dozen times. Why, just last winter I was exposed to hepatitis while I was workin' over at the fairgrounds." He shook his head. "Nothin' serious, though. A couple of shots and they took care of it. But I've been worried about Martha."

David nodded sympathetically. "You've got a nice place here. Had any trouble with the fruit fly?"

"Thank the Lord for small favors, no. The spraying took care of the fruit flies, I guess. We didn't even have to pick off the fruit this time because they got started spraying so early."

The horses were shifting restlessly. Janina spoke. "Next time you go to visit Martha, if you like, stop in my office and we'll go up and see her together. She is in satisfactory condition, though, and I'm sure your doctor would tell you if there was any need for concern."

He seemed satisfied and they said goodbye, then prodded the horses toward the path that led to a grove of eucalyptus trees some distance across an open space dotted with boulders and well-established growths of Monterey pine. Partly hidden by the rise of trees and the beginning swell of the foothill range of the Santa Cruz Mountains, Janina saw the squared-off buildings that housed Langtree Labs. One tower rose above the rest. It was new and glistening white against the mauve and soft tans of the foothills that rose behind it.

She felt the tiny hairs rise up on her arms despite the warmth of the late-afternoon sun. "Look, David. There it is."

"Looks innocent enough, doesn't it?"

"Maybe. But looks deceive." She let her horse drop back alongside his. "I was just thinking. It's funny, isn't it, that the pancreatitis is so selective. Why does it attack some people and not others?"

He shrugged. "Probably a question of resistance."

"Oh, come on, David. You heard Mr. Gartner. Martha was as healthy as a horse."

"How many people have said the same thing, only to drop dead a few weeks later?"

She shifted the reins to her other hand and leaned forward to rest her hands on the pommel. "I know what you say is true but—"

"But we have to try to weigh all possibilities. I'm not arguing with you, Janina. All we have now is a theory that they are manufacturing a spray out here that is being used instead of the malathion. Without something better than that, it's too thin to be evidence. We've got to come up with something more valid."

"But how?"

"We'll think of a way."

They continued on in silence until they reached the place David selected for their picnic. Once there, David tethered the horses while Janina found a spot to spread the blanket. The scent of eucalyptus hung heavy in the afternoon air and high above the moss-green leaves of the trees, a red-tailed hawk drifted on warm currents of air wafted in from the distant Pacific.

When he had finished his sandwich, David lay back on the blanket and looked up at the thin ribbon of a jet stream crossing the sky. It looked so clean, so pristine-white against the azure blue. Another part of him was aware that Janina was watching him. She had matured into an exciting woman; confident, capable and extremely desirable. He reached over and patted the blanket next to him. Another woman might have played the reluctant game, but she came to him willingly. . . no pretense, just honest and straightforward. He loved that about her.

She lay back and rested her head on the curve of his arm. "This was a terrific idea, David. I really needed it after the day I had at the hospital."

Still supporting her head on his arm, he rolled over to face her. "I think we both need it, Janina."

Her eyes opened wide as she looked up at him, so close that she saw her desire mirrored in his gaze. He bent over her, nuzzling her cheek with his nose. "I've needed you more than you can ever guess. More than I care to admit."

She reached up and pulled his mouth down to hers, kissing him deeply, without restraint. The sun's heat through the branches of the eucalyptus tree warmed his back. Sensing an even greater warmth, Janina slid her hands under his shirt and traced the corded muscles beneath the smooth skin. He moaned against her mouth as his tongue began a frenzied probing.

Her hands slid downward along the ridge of his spine, then skirted the waistband of his jeans to come together above the hard, muscular surface of his abdomen. With gentle flutterings of her fingers, she discovered his navel and explored it with seductive strokes of her thumb and forefinger.

David caught her bottom lip between his and teased it with his tongue, then kissed her with ever-increasing forcefulness until her senses were swept up in a whirlwind of sensuality. His hands encircled her waist, then slid forward to burrow beneath her lacy bra. With a sigh of satisfaction, he stroked the undersides of her breasts with his thumbs.

"God, Janina. You have the most beautiful skin. I can't get enough of it." He buried his head between her breasts and brushed his tongue along the smooth curves.

Janina sensed the last bit of her resistance beginning to slip away. She wanted to yield to him in every way. To touch him, to hold him, to feel him inside her.

He kissed her again, softly on the mouth. Then as they lay there, his hand moved to her chin and she felt his finger trace the inner curve of her lips, probing them open until it was inside. She touched it with her tongue, tentatively at first, then with greater abandon. His mouth descended again and this time the urgency in his kiss was not to be denied. She hesitated for a bare instant. Then a core of heat deep inside her seemed to burst with desire.

Suddenly he tore himself away and rolled over to look up at the sky. "Next time we plan a picnic, it's going to be on a deserted island. I'm getting too old to make love in the open air with all the world looking on."

She laughed shakily. "Your head may be old, but your body isn't." She turned her head to watch him. "I'm sorry, David. I didn't mean to lead you on, or anything."

He caught her hand and pressed it to his lips. "Don't say anything to spoil my illusions. I'm trying to tell myself that you still love me."

"David..."

"Not now. Let's talk about something else."

This was a different David. More vulnerable, tender. She didn't know how to handle it. They lay there for a minute staring at the sky. Suddenly David broke the silence.

"So what happened at the hospital?"

She started laughing, but it was less from humor than a letting down of tension and as her laughter died, tears stung her eyes. "I'm afraid we're going to lose one of our pancreatitis patients. He started hemorrhaging today and they had to take him to OR."

David touched her shoulder. "Put it out of your mind for a while. You can't let it get to you, Janina. You have to learn to divorce yourself from it or you'll burn out."

"I thought I'd learned how, but this epidemic...I can't get it out of my mind."

"We can't accurately call it an epidemic, not yet anyway."

"I can. It is, as far as I'm concerned."

"But you're just a glorified—"

She rolled over and started pounding his chest. "David Madison, if you quote that damned administrator another time, I'm going to—"

"What?" he murmured against her cheek as he pulled her head down to his face.

"Ask me another time," she whispered. Their eyes were open and she saw the sun and tree shadows touching his face as they kissed. It seemed right being here with him, close, touching, feeling the warmth of his body from his demanding mouth down the long length of him. He snugged her hips against him and rolled over until she was on the bottom and he could see the sun glinting the gold in her hair.

His mouth sought the hollow of her throat. "Janina,

my love. It's been such a long time." Her hands cupped his face as her thumbs traced the contour of his shaggy brows.

"I know, but I can't, David. Not yet."

He sat up slowly, without anger. "I think maybe we'd better go, Janina. The stable will close in a couple of hours."

She opened her eyes and looked at him in surprise. "But it's only a twenty-minute ride at best."

"We'll need the extra time to get a closer look at the lab."

She sat up quickly. "Do you think we can?"

"We'll sure try. The electric fence is closer to the buildings here than it is anywhere else. See that square tower? It looks like a guard tower to me, but the chance that they would be watching this direction is very remote."

"You mean we could have been seen when we almost..."

David grinned. "But we didn't. At this particular minute, though, I feel like it would have been worth it."

Janina smiled. She knew better than to deny it. David understood her far too well.

By the time they repacked the picnic gear, the horses were ready to leave. They seemed to sense that they were on the last lap and it wasn't necessary to prod them forward.

Ten minutes later, they had reached the outside perimeter of the electric fence. The buildings were still a good distance away and partially hidden by new growth of scrub and high grasses. But it was close enough to give them a clear view of what was happening.

She sucked in her breath. "My God, David. It looks like pictures I've seen of the moon landing."

David swore softly. "What the hell is going on over there?"

They stared at four men who were dressed from head to foot in bulky white protective clothing that resembled space suits. Each man carried a large canister of some sort on his back and appeared to be spraying the outside of a semidetached building and an extensive area immediately surrounding it.

Janina drew a deep breath and started to say something but began coughing. "Ugh." She made a face. "It's that cloyingly sweet smell again."

David sniffed experimentally. "Licorice?"

"It's the same thing I smelled when the spray planes flew over. Sickening. I can't stand it."

"That means there has to be a definite tie-in to the fruit-fly problem. Maybe they really are manufacturing the spray here at the lab. Do you remember what was in this wing?"

Janina shook her head. "I'm not sure. This wing is so much larger than it was when I was out here with Gary. It could be the new-products lab."

"Let's move up a little and try to get a better look."

As they turned the horses east to follow along the fence, Janina noticed an even more intense smell. "Oh, God, David. It's a dead racoon."

"Stay away from it."

"Don't worry. I had no intention of touching it. Let's move on before I get sick. I can't get the smells out of my head."

"Would a drink of coffee help? I kept the thermos out of the basket," he said, holding up a quart-size dark cylinder.

"Thanks, but I don't think I could—"

Before she could finish, David interrupted. "Uh oh.

Big Brother up in the tower just spotted us. I saw the sunlight flash on something moving behind those glass windows. They must be using binoculars. We'd better get ourselves out of here.''

He swung his horse around in the direction of the stables and Janina followed close behind. They had gone no more than a few hundred feet when a pair of city policemen cut across the field on motorcycles and headed toward them.

David blew his breath out slowly. "We've had it now. Look, Janina. Don't say a thing about what we saw. We're on a picnic. That's all.''

She nodded, feeling her heart thump against her ribs. She was too scared to do anything else.

Had it not been for the Willowbrook Police Department insignia emblazoned across the front of the motorcycles, the two men in their black leather jackets, black visored helmets and black leather gloves might have been members of some outlaw motorcycle gang. Their one redeeming quality, as far as Janina could tell from a distance, was that they cut their engines and parked their bikes far enough away that they didn't scare the horses. She hugged that comforting thought to her chest. But as they approached, she found her confidence begin to slip.

Chapter Six

They spoke to David first, but their gaze constantly monitored Janina's actions and anything else that might be moving within a few hundred yards.

The taller one seemed to be in charge. "Would you kindly get down and show some identification, sir, ma'am?"

David grinned. "I give up. What is it? Speeding? Illegal parking?" He slid down and started to take out his wallet, but the cop spoke harshly.

"Over here, please. On this side of the horses so we can see what you're doing."

David obliged and handed them his driver's license. Janina took hers out of the plastic enclosure and gave it to the other man.

The first one jotted something down in a notebook. Then he took Janina's license and wrote again. When he finished he looked up. "May I ask what you're doing here?"

"Certainly. We've been horseback riding. Then we stopped for a picnic over there in the eucalyptus grove, after which we went horseback riding again."

"Why over here? The trails are all along the road. Not by the fence."

Janina smiled as innocently as possible. "We thought maybe we could find a shorter trail. The stable's going to close in a few minutes. Was the property posted? We didn't think we were trespassing."

"It's private property, Miss...uh." He looked at his notebook. "Miss Scott."

The other officer was walking around the horses, carefully looking them over. "What's this?" he asked, holding up the black rubber-covered thermos bottle.

"Just a thermos of coffee. I told you we were on a picnic."

The officer put it back and walked over to join the more aggressive policeman, who snapped his notebook shut.

"In the future we would appreciate it if you would please confine your riding to the proper paths." His voice softened, but the cold, unrelenting expression stayed in his eyes and Janina was reminded of a reptile watching an unwary prey.

David replaced his wallet. "Sure, no problem."

Janina was dying to ask if they knew what was going on over at the labs, but one look at David's face and she clamped her mouth shut. They didn't say another word until the officers had mounted their bikes. The two men sat waiting while Janina and David rode back to the lane and turned in the direction of the stables.

Janina looked at David. "Are they gone? I'm afraid to turn around."

"They're gone. What I want to know is, who sent them?"

She heard the tightness in his voice and saw the drawn expression around his eyes. "You don't believe it was just a coincidence that they stopped us, do you, David?"

"Not for a minute."

"Then it had to be someone from Langtree Laboratories. But why?"

"Why else? Either they think that we might be in some danger of contamination from the spray on the foliage over here or...? I don't know. One thing for sure. They don't want anyone snooping around."

Janina was silent. After what seemed like minutes, she looked steadily in front of her. "They know who we are, now...and where I live."

David recognized the apprehension in her voice and he wanted to reassure her. "Look, it's probably nothing. I'm sure we don't have anything to worry about as long as—"

"As long as we keep our mouths shut and don't stir up any trouble over the spray. You don't have to soothe me, David," she said sharply. "I'm frightened, I admit it. But I'm more afraid of what's happening here in Willowbrook and the fact that nobody is willing to talk about it. I may be scared as the devil, but I'm not stopping now, not until we get somebody to admit the truth."

He looked over at her and smiled. "Somehow I suspected you wouldn't. I just hope you aren't going to take on more than you can handle."

They kept going over the same conversational ground even after they got into the car and headed back toward Janina's condominium. Finally, Janina abruptly sat up and turned toward David, her voice earnest, tight with emotion.

"Come on, David. Let's hurry. I've made up my mind. I'm going to call the police and tell them what we know."

"I think you'd be making a big mistake. Langtree is

an influential name in Willowbrook. It's Langtree Industries that's keeping this town alive and fighting
them is like taking on city hall. In the true sense of the
word, they own the town.''

"I know what you say is right, but I have to make
the effort.'' She slammed her fist against her open
palm. "We keep talking about doing something, but
so far it's just talk. I think it's time we act and the only
thing I can think of is to go to the police with what we
know.''

"All right. If that's the way you feel. Would you
like me to pull over right now and save you the trip
downtown?''

"What?''

"All we have to do is pull over to the curb.'' His
gaze left the street and glanced in the rearview mirror.
"Don't look back, but a squad car has been discreetly
following us almost since we left the stables.''

"Oh, God! I can't believe this is happening. What
are we going to do?'' Her mouth had suddenly gone
dry and she ran her tongue across her lips to moisten
them. "You—you'd think we were the criminals. This
is getting to be a nightmare.''

"I have a feeling that we haven't seen anything yet.
Are you sure you want to get more involved?''

"I have to, David. But you don't. I won't be angry
or anything if you want to keep out of it.''

He looked over at her as he pulled into the parking
space at the condominium and turned off the ignition.
"I'd say we're in this together, love.''

Janina felt a surge of warmth engulf her. She started
to reach out to him, but at that moment the police
cruiser coasted by and she wanted nothing more than
to get away from them, get out of their sight.

The telephone was ringing when she unlocked the apartment. Janina ran into the den and grabbed it. "Janina Scott."

"Janina, this is Sandy Hobart from ICU. You asked me to let you know if we lost any of our pancreatitis patients." She paused and Janina chilled all the way to the bone before Sandy continued.

"I wish I had good news. You know about George Murdock from 309 West?"

"Yes. He came up from Recovery last week. Same room as Vince Costello."

"Right. He expired about an hour ago. They tried everything—took him back to OR, the works. But it was no go. Sorry. I thought you would want me to tell you."

"I—yes, Sandy. I appreciate your call."

"If it's any consolation, Janina. There are a lot of us here at the hospital who are beginning to agree with you. We're just too cowardly to face up to anybody. We've got kids to think of, you know?"

Janina nodded. "I know, Sandy. And believe me, I do understand. Thanks, though, and please keep me posted, will you?"

"Count on it."

Janina stood there holding the receiver for several minutes after Sandy hung up. She couldn't blame Sandy and the others for refusing to speak up but on the other hand, what about their obligation to their patients? It made her sick to think that lives were being put in jeopardy because nurses were afraid for their job security.

David strode across the room when he saw Janina's face, then took the receiver from her and put it back in the cradle.

"My God, Janina, what is it?" he demanded. At first he thought something had happened to her parents. She was so white, so stiff, she looked frozen. He turned her around and took her into his arms. Her body melted against him as she buried her head on his chest, trembling as if shaken to the core of her being.

"Tell me, love. Tell me what's happened," he murmured against her hair.

Janina fought the tears that burned in her throat. "They lost a patient in OR. I wonder who else they will let die before they admit something is wrong?"

"We need proof, Janina. Solid proof that nobody can deny or cover up."

"But we can't get into the lab. They'll be watching for someone to break in now that they know we were there."

"I know. We have to think of another way."

"I'm so frightened, I can't think straight. David?" She looked up at him, her eyes luminous with tears. "David, would you stay with me? Move in until this is all over? I can make up the bed in the den. I—I need someone around to talk to."

"Sure. I'll go over and check out of the motel."

"You don't mind?"

He grinned. "Does Christmas come in December? Promise me one thing, though. Don't do any cooking until I get back. I'll cook, you wash dishes. Is it a deal?"

She nodded then reached up to cup his face in her hands. "In some ways, you are a pretty terrific guy, David Madison. If...if I haven't told you before...I'm glad you came back."

His eyes became noticeably moist. He bent quickly and covered her mouth with a searching kiss that soothed the raw edges of her nerves like cooling lotion on sunburned skin. She relaxed in his arms, letting her fingers ignite ribbons of fire along his cheek, down the curve of his throat to the place where his shirt opened to his collarbone. He sighed against her cheek.

"Oh, Janina. When we are together like this it seems as if time doesn't exist. If only we could take up where we left off and forget those two years."

"It's not that easy, David."

"I know, love. I know. But we'll work it out. We have to."

Reluctantly he released her. She didn't walk to his car; it would have destroyed the beauty of the moment. But she watched him go down the walk and cross the lawn to the parking area. After he left, she tried to analyze her feelings. She had surprised even herself by asking David to move in with her. Had she done so simply because she was frightened, or was there a far deeper reason? She wanted to be honest with herself, but she wasn't quite ready to answer that particular question.

It was surprisingly comforting to have David settled in as a guest in her house. Janina had expected it to be awkward at times, but he made no demands on her; instead, he seemed to go out of his way to make her feel at ease. As for David, he had mixed emotions. This was what he wanted, or almost. He would have liked to have been there under different circumstances, but he was willing to accept her terms. It gave him a chance to be near her and that's all he could expect from Janina right now. He groaned and rolled over. Life wasn't easy sometimes.

Janina had gone to bed early that night, comforted by his nearness but restless, knowing he was in the same house, sleeping alone in his bed just a few precious feet from where she lay. More than once she was tempted to go to him, but she was still too insecure about his feelings toward her.

JANINA WASN'T THRILLED with the idea of going to work the next day but with the patient load at a peak, she knew she would have her work stacked to the ceiling. Several of the floors were using hall stations to house patients, and even in OB there seemed to be more than the usual number of births. Once she got into the swing of things, the day moved well and once, for one whole hour, she was able to put David out of her mind completely.

She had just gotten home from work and was telling David about her day as they watched a game show on the television when an announcer interrupted the regular program with a newsbreak. "Harvey Rudolph, of the Department of Agriculture and director of the campaign to eradicate the fruit fly, announced today in a meeting at city hall, that a stepped-up spray program will begin today. Residents in the area west of Capitol should be advised that spraying will begin on a nightly basis between the hours of nine and eleven-thirty."

"That includes us," Janina said.

They listened silently as the announcer interviewed one of the fruit growers who seemed highly pleased with the decision. He spoke glowingly of the campaign director.

"No, sir. I tell you this time they know what they're doin'. I've been checkin' the traps every day and still haven't found a fruit fly. Now last time, I had to pick and burn the whole crop, the flies was so bad. I'm behind them a hundred percent."

Another grower had much the same thing to say about it. Then the special news program ended and the station went back to its scheduled game show.

"Do you believe that?" Janina asked, turning off the remote-control switch.

He shook his head.

She curled her feet up under her legs as she stroked Cinnamon's back. "I just thought of something. Mr. Gartner, you know, the man who was watering his fruit trees out near the stable? He said the same thing. He hasn't seen any fruit flies, either. Don't you find that strange?"

David nodded. "Well, what say we drive out and visit some of the growers and see what kind of story *they* have to tell."

"I don't know what good it's going to do, but I'm with you."

The first thing David noticed when he got into the Mercedes after closing her door, was that Janina was sitting in the middle. *Progress,* he thought. *She really does still care about me.* As he backed the car up and turned toward the foothills, her hip grazed his and the warmth of it shot all the way up to his Adam's apple.

Janina was beginning to accept him again. True, she hadn't committed herself in so many words, but he thought that she was mellowing, maybe had been for a day or two. It was hard to tell now. She had learned to cover her feelings well, maybe too well. He was partly responsible for that. Three years ago she had been as open and trusting as a little girl. That was when they were seeing each other. She used to say what was on her mind where her emotions were concerned. More than once they had been sitting on the sofa in her old apartment and she would look up at him and say, "Make love to me, David. I need you."

But it was different now. She was her own woman. She didn't need anyone. In some ways, that was good but it was sad, too, that single-minded self-reliance that she wore like a suit of armor. He wanted her to need him, wanted things to be like they were between them before he married Susan. *Face it, man,* he thought. *You want to make love to her, but you want more than that, much more.*

Janina interrupted his thoughts. "We ought to be able to visit two fruit growers who have orchards right here in the foothills. I found their addresses in the phone book."

"We passed one on the way back from Langtree Labs last night."

"That reminds me. Have you seen anything more of the police car that was cruising around my area?"

He shook his head. "No. But I was pretty busy working on some reports. I hope you're not worried about them. We haven't done anything illegal. They can't do a thing to us."

Janina patted his leg. "Oh, David. It's so good having you on my side."

He grinned. "My side feels pretty good, too. It'll feel even better if you move a little closer."

He was surprised when she laughed and snuggled closer. *Progress,* he thought contentedly, and settled back against the seat.

A short time later they spotted the sign pointing to the main building for Norton Farms, Leading Growers and Packagers of Apricots and Peaches, and turned into the lane.

J. K. Norton was just slightly less than jubilant about the stepped-up campaign to eradicate the fruit fly. He considered himself among the lucky ones to have escaped an infestation this time. Last time, he had lost almost fifty thousand dollars to the Medfly. He couldn't survive another such loss. The two other growers they visited that afternoon said basically the same thing.

As they got back into the Mercedes, Janina put her arm across the back of the seat and turned toward David. "I've had it, how about you?"

"Up to here. So far we haven't met a single person who has found fruit flies in any of the traps."

"The new spray must really be effective."

"But who's willing to pay the price?" David asked. "And why doesn't anyone just come out and admit that the spray is not malathion?"

"Maybe they know it's untested and dangerous. But if that's true, then the public has a right to know what chances they're taking." Janina watched David's face to gauge his reaction. "I think we need to get a sample of the spray."

He laughed aloud. "Good luck. Just how do you plan to do that? You going to stand out under the helicopters with your little specimen bottle and wait for them to fill it? This isn't exactly outpatient clinic time at the hospital."

"There has to be a way. All we have to do is find it."

They were silent as they drove back to the condominium. Once inside her apartment, Janina faced David and put her hands on his arms. "Listen. If I get a sample of the new insecticide they're using, could you get it analyzed?"

"Well. . . I'm not sure but I think I know a guy who still works at one of the local labs. Yes, I think I could handle it."

She threw her arms around him and hugged. "Oh, David. I knew I could count on you."

He hugged her for a moment, then held her at arm's length. Their gaze met and then they forgot to look because he was kissing her and she was kissing him and their eyes were closed. It wasn't a big passionate thing. It was more like a "glad to be alive and here in the same place with you" kiss.

Janina felt like a kid out of school. Young, happy-go-lucky, full of the joy of having David back even for a short time.

David was overcome with her eagerness to be in his arms. It filled him with an infinite gladness to know that she had begun to trust him once again.

It was only then that he remembered what had triggered her exuberance. "Wait, Janina. Before we get carried away, maybe you'd better tell me just how you plan to get the sample of insecticide."

"I don't have the whole thing worked out, but it shouldn't be too hard. Remember the newscast, when they were talking about a staging area? That has to be where the helicopters take on their loads of insecticide."

"I'll go along with that, but if you think you can march right up there with your plastic bleach bottle and say 'fill it up,' you're in for a surprise."

"Idiot. I'll just sneak in between helicopters and fill it up myself. After dark, no one will see me. There's sure to be a pause between helicopters. I hardly think they'll lock up the pumps or whatever they use until they're all finished for the night."

He turned away and walked toward the fish tank, staring down into the miniature shipwreck where an angelfish nibbled at a bit of algae.

"I don't know, Janina. We'd be taking a big chance. If we get caught, they'll arrest us for sure."

"At least we'd get the public's attention."

"You can count on it." He stroked his chin. "All right. We'll see if we can find the staging area, then check out the surroundings. If it looks safe, we'll do it."

Janina stood behind him and held him against her. "Thanks, David. I knew you would."

He reached for her hands and brushed his lips against them. "My guess is that we're both slightly crazy and we're going to live to regret it, love."

"Don't even think that way." She rested her head against his back, letting his strength flow into her. There was no doubt in her mind that they could do it. With David beside her, anything was possible.

DARKNESS CAME before they were ready for it. The site of the staging ground for the helicopters wasn't public information, as they thought it would be. Instead, they were forced to use the process of elimination. Whatever happened, if and when they found the location, they were determined to go through with their plan. They wore dark clothing and carried surgical gloves to protect their hands from the chemical. David turned in the direction of the foothills.

"We know they come from the east, then make the turn at the beach and fly back," David said. "I suspect that they want to spray with the wind so the insecticide carries to the area they intend to cover."

"But why wouldn't they have the staging ground on the west side of town, toward the beach?"

"Too populated. If I remember correctly, there's a public utility storage yard located out at the end of Canyon Drive. If my hunch is right, that's where we'll find them."

"Was it really necessary for us to dress all in black?" Janina asked. "I feel like a female James Bond."

"If we have to go in under cover of darkness when there are people in the area, we'll be a lot less visible. Besides," he said, grinning, "you look terrific in black jeans and that black turtleneck sweater."

"It's like wearing a plastic raincoat on a sweltering hot day. I'm drenched with perspiration."

"Nerves."

"Probably, but I can't wait to get home and take a shower. I'm beginning to itch."

"We're almost there. You've got the bottles?"

"Yes," Janina said. "The tops aren't as large as I'd like, but they're better than bleach bottles."

He slowed the car to a crawl and turned off the headlights. Immediately they were engulfed in darkness. The road was completely deserted and the moon, when it came out from under a dense cover of clouds, gave mute testimony to the fact that the county storage facility was not the place they were looking for.

"Damn!" David swore softly. "Now where the devil can we look for the staging ground? I know they came from this direction. I was so sure—"

He was interrupted by the distant flutter of the chopper rotors. Janina put her hand on his arm.

"That's them, David. Listen." Her heart rose up in her throat as her body tensed. "I think they're coming this way."

He swung the Mercedes around and let the motor idle. "All right. We'll follow them. They must be coming in for fuel or a refill of the insecticide."

It seemed like an eternity before the single beam of the lead helicopter's light came into view. Janina sucked in her breath. "They're going to see us. They're coming this way."

David reached for her hand. "Easy, love. The trees provide plenty of cover. If they were looking for us, it might be different. All they care about is getting their job done."

Janina let her breath slowly escape as the four helicopters came in low, then passed overhead like a formation of giant-winged locusts. The sound was overwhelming. She felt it fluttering her lungs and compressing her eardrums as it sent waves of distress through her nervous system.

"Whose idea was this?" she asked as the helicopters passed over the treetops.

"Look. I think they're landing." He eased the car into a sharp turn and drove in the direction they disappeared, listening for the source of the noise of the engines, which had diminished to a soft flutter. "What else is down this way?"

"Nothing I can think of." She sorted through bits and pieces of trivia stored in her brain. "I think there might have been a fire department training camp out here, but it was a long time ago. One of the buildings burned down."

"City-owned property. That just might be the place. I'm going to drive with my lights off pretty soon, so hold on. It could be bumpy."

When the moon slipped free of the clouds, there was enough light to illuminate the sliver of road, which was bordered on each side by pepper trees and sun-dried undergrowth. David hit a pothole and the car thumped a protest somewhere beneath the carpeted floorboards.

"Look. There it is." David whistled softly. "Two tanker trucks and they're both hooked up to the choppers. I think we're in luck."

Janina wasn't so sure. The closer she got to actually going through with her plan, the less convinced she was that it was a good idea. But David was caught up in it. Even in the faint light from the dash, she could see the excitement in his eyes. This was a side of his personality she hadn't expected. He had courage; she would never doubt that. But was there also a touch of foolhardiness?

He slowed down, cut the engine and coasted to a stop in a cluster of trees. "I think it's too risky to drive beyond this point. We'll have to wait for the copters to leave before we go in, but I want to get as close as we can under cover of their noise when they take off."

Janina looked at him in wonder. "You sound like a Marine sergeant going out on patrol."

"Keep your voice down or you'll think the Marines have landed on us. Listen, Janina. One of us is all it takes to get in, get a sample of the stuff and get out. You wait in the car while I take care of it."

"Not on your life, Buster."

"But I think—"

"I said no, David."

"All right, love." He leaned over and kissed her squarely on the mouth. "You be careful out there and don't take any chances. If we get separated, you head for the car. There's an extra key under the door upholstery. Here. If anything happens that I get caught, you take the car and get the hell out of here."

"Will you promise to do the same if I get caught?"

"That's different."

"Like hell it is. The same rules go for both of us. It makes sense to have at least one person get away. That's why we brought two bottles." She leaned toward him until he could see the moon reflected in the deep blue of her eyes. "David, stop trying to change the plan at this stage in the operation. It's just going to muck things up.''

He nodded. "All right. Be careful, Janina." He kissed her again and she sensed an urgency that went beyond mere physical needs. She wanted to pursue the thought, but something was happening in the small circle of light that surrounded the helicopters. She tensed.

"Look. I think the men are unhooking the hoses. They must be about ready to make another run."

David looked at her. "I just thought of something. The damn lights are going to come on when we open the door."

"Can you take the bulb out?"

He reached up by the rearview mirror and flipped a switch. "I turned out the dome light, but the door lights are bound to come on. I can't open them up without a screwdriver."

"Then smash the damn covers."

"It's not that easy. We'll just have to open and close the doors quickly. I think the trees will give us enough cover that no one will see us."

Janina's heart was thumping against her chest wall as she grabbed the plastic bottles. Her breath came in short gasps through her mouth and she had to swallow twice to keep her throat from drying out.

The sound of the doors closing was like a small explosion. Fortunately, the increasing roar of the helicopter engines drowned any noise the two of them were making.

"Follow me," David whispered, taking one of the bottles from her and grabbing her hand. He skirted the edge of the road, then cut through an opening in the underbrush and headed toward the dense cover that grew close to the chain-link fence gate. He stumbled once and she thought he would fall, but his grip tightened and he righted himself.

They stopped just ten feet short of the gate in a pine thicket created by an aging, gnarled tree that hung over the fence. The voices, if there were any, were masked by the sound of the engines. Two helicopters had finished refilling the insecticide chambers and the other two had people working on them. Janina saw eight men in all. How many of them would leave with the helicopters, she had no idea. And that was the problem. She had heard that the helicopters sometimes carried a second man to ride shotgun since some of the irate local citizens had taken potshots at the helicopters, using everything from slingshots to rifles. If that were true, it would leave at the most, two men on the ground.

Her body was drenched with sweat, but at the same time she was trembling with the cold. David pulled her close against him and she was grateful for the human contact.

"Better put on the gloves," he said.

She nodded and with considerable difficulty, slipped on a pair of thin surgical gloves. David leaned toward her ear. "Next time, we'll do this in the car."

Her giggle betrayed a note of hysteria. David squeezed her arm reassuringly.

"I think they're about ready to take off. Remember what I told you, love, and be careful."

Two men backed away from the rotor blades and stood at a distance, their hands shoved in the pockets of their jeans, as the helicopters lifted off, then moved into a sort of formation in the direction of the foothills. For a few minutes the men stood beside one of the tanker trucks and talked. Then, apparently knowing there would be a long wait until the helicopters returned, they got into one of the trucks and closed the door. Minutes later Janina heard the nasal voice of a disk jockey float across the night air.

David whispered. "It's going to be easier than we thought. This is the best chance we'll ever get. You ready?"

Janina took a deep breath. "Let's go."

"Stay close behind me."

"Don't worry, I will."

A single drop light on an arm extending outward from a water tower afforded enough light for them to locate the nozzle that was used to fill the tanks mounted on the belly of the helicopter. David avoided the circle of light until they were out of the line of vision of the men in the truck. The radio blared a country-and-western song, effectively covering the noise David and Janina made as they crossed a stretch of gravel. Once they located the nozzle, it took only seconds for them to fill the wide-mouth bottles, but to Janina it felt like ten minutes.

She swore softly. "I can't get this damn lid to screw on. The gloves—"

David traded bottles with her. "Okay. That does it. Let's get out of here."

The trip back to the car seemed twice as long as it had before. Janina dared a single glance behind her, but no one had followed.

When they were back in the car with the bottles stowed safely in the trunk, their surgical gloves disposed of in a pile of forest debris, they looked at each other and started to laugh.

"We did it, David. I can't believe we actually did it without getting caught."

He started to say something when the headlight

beams of an oncoming car flooded the area with light. David grabbed her and pulled her against him before she had a chance to say anything. He murmured against her mouth.

"This is what they do in all the spy movies, isn't it, when they're afraid of getting caught?"

"Um," Janina said. Her eyes were open just long enough to see the car move on by without even slowing down. Then she closed her eyes and gave herself over to the absolute pleasure of his kiss.

It was a heady sensation. She was aware of twin dangers; the very real threat of discovery and the danger that lay in David's kiss. It heightened her sensitivity to what was happening and she savored the moment, filled with the anticipation of an Olympic diver standing poised for the high dive. When he finally backed away, Janina opened her eyes and spoke with unaccustomed huskiness.

"I think we handled that pretty well."

"Getting the sample, or the passing car?"

"Definitely."

David laughed and straightened. "Maybe we'd better leave while we're ahead."

It took a while for the giddy sensation to settle into a nice satisfying glow of success. Janina felt for the first time that they were making some sort of progress in their effort to prove that the spray was not the relatively harmless malathion it was claimed to be. David felt he was making progress in other directions no less important to him than the safety of the community.

As she moved across the seat to sit close to him, Janina laughed. "This has to be the most daring thing I've done since some of us student nurses put our instructor's sweater on the skeleton in our anatomy class."

David grinned. "We put erotic pictures on the slides in our biology class."

"Did you get caught?"

"Yes."

"I'm sorry I asked."

While David dropped the sample off at the lab where his friend worked, Janina waited in the car. David explained that it was an unauthorized analysis and the fewer people directly involved, the less dangerous it would be for his friend.

"How soon will it be ready?" Janina asked as David got back into the car.

"He couldn't say. It depends on how complex the formula is. He'll do his best. At least we should learn pretty soon whether or not it's malathion." David hooked his fingers over the steering wheel. "Ready to go home?"

Janina nodded. "This sweater scratches."

He plucked a leaf from her hair and flicked it out the window. "I'm going to hit the shower the minute I walk in the door."

"Me, too. I don't think I'm cut out for the commando business, sneaking through the bushes and all that. It's a good thing I have two showers, so that we don't have to take turns."

"We wouldn't."

Janina slanted a look at him. "Don't push your luck, Buster." She wasn't angry with him. She was feeling so on top of everything, so euphoric that she was convinced nothing could spoil it.

Strange, looking across at David she felt almost married to him. It was hard to make herself believe that in a few short weeks he would be going back to San Diego. He was becoming increasingly important to her. Too much so, for her own peace of mind. But she pushed the thought out of her head. Tonight seemed like an escapade, now that it was over, and she didn't want anything to spoil their mood.

They spent the first part of the evening listening for news reports on television to see if anything new had happened concerning the fruit-fly invasion. Most of the coverage touched on the humorous side: the T-shirts proclaiming I Survived the Fruit Fly and Spray It Again, Sam. A few interviews gave the side of the concerned citizen, but the interviewer managed to include a few wackos such as the woman who claimed she had flown in from Venus and was responsible for the fruit-fly invasion.

Janina had put on a vibrant turquoise and metallic gold caftan and wrapped her hair in a cerise towel while she watched the news. But her thoughts were on David. He looked. . .she searched for a work to describe him and came up with *tempting*. His black hair glistened from the shower. He was tucking his shirt into his brown trousers as he came into the room and the ivory silk against the dark cushion of hair on his chest made her want to lay her cheek against it.

He sat down in the big armchair in the living room and motioned to the ottoman next to it. "Come on. Sit down there and I'll towel your hair dry."

She knew it wasn't a good idea, but she was powerless to resist. He smelled clean and wet from the shower. It triggered memories of other times he had stayed with her, making it impossible to keep any kind of perspective.

Chapter Seven

"Lean back, Janina. I can't reach the towel." She moved against him, into the curve of his thighs, and was warmed by the heat of his body. His fingers unwrapped the towel and began a slow, sensuous massage that electrified her nerve-endings until she was hypnotized by the lovely sensations.

He coaxed her farther back until she was lying against him, completely bedazzled by the magic his hands were working on her head and neck and shoulders. She was curiously aware that his body, too, had quickened with an undeniable urgency and it served to heighten her own sensitivity. Each breath, each movement seemed to draw them closer to some preprogrammed culmination of emotions.

Somewhere along the way, he forgot that he was drying her hair. He held her in his arms, his lips touching her hair, her face, her eyebrows. She was beautiful without makeup. He loved the clean-scrubbed look that made her face glow with energy and good health.

She turned her face up to his and he kissed her, then murmured against her mouth. "We could be more comfortable in your bedroom."

She smiled. "I'm already too comfortable to move."

"Terrific." His tone was dry but she knew he wasn't angry. She reached up and pulled his head down to her level, then kissed him with all the skill at her command. He swore softly. "I know someone who's asking for trouble."

"Want me to move?"

He hesitated and Janina looked up at him with a questioning glance. He shook his head. "Don't rush me. I'm trying to decide how much punishment I can take."

It was a television newscaster who broke the mood with his announcement. "Word has just reached the station that a helicopter is down in a wooded lot near the intersection of Mesquite and Fullerton streets. The two-man crew has escaped without injury and damage to the aircraft is slight. At least one eyewitness claims that sniper fire was responsible for the crash, but another source says that a rotor blade clipped a telephone line. Earlier, a late-model car was spotted near the helicopter staging grounds, but so far there is no reported connection between the two incidents."

Janina sat up. "Was that your car they were talking about?"

He sighed. "Janina, my love. At this moment I couldn't care less."

Janina was torn. A part of her wanted to take up where they left off. Another part of her was grateful for the chance to come to her senses. Having David in the house contributed little to her emotional stability. Not that he would attack her. It wasn't him she was afraid of; it was her own lack of self-control.

"I'm sorry, David. I . . ."

He shrugged. "Look, forget it. Trying to explain it away is only going to make it worse. I think I'm going to call it a night."

She stood for a moment looking at him. Trying to read in his eyes, in the sound of his voice, how he really felt about her. He wanted her, there was no question about that. What she wanted to know was how badly he wanted her...and for how long? He stopped what he was doing and returned her gaze. It, too, questioned.

She turned away, no longer able to face him. "Good night, David."

"Good night, love." His voice was soft, forgiving. She had expected anger or, at the very least, irritation. It made it even more difficult to close the door to her bedroom and leave him outside.

It wasn't that late. Knowing that her mother was a night owl, Janina called to see how things were. Her mother told her that Debbie had been seeing Doug again and things were running a bit more smoothly. Janina was profoundly relieved. At least one part of her life had begun to go right.

"And what have you been up to, Janina?" her mother asked.

"I—well I—" She nearly started to laugh. "As a matter of fact, I just got back from a commando raid on a fire station."

"Janina Scott! Sometimes your sense of humor is so outlandish! Have you and David Madison been partying?"

"Mother! You know me better than that."

"Of course, dear. It was just a joke. You're so dependable, I never have to lose sleep over you." Janina heard her cluck like a mother hen. "Now, tell David he's welcome to come visit."

"Yes, Mother. When the time is right. Sleep well and give my love to Dad and Deb."

Janina didn't sleep well that night. David was restless

and she could hear him prowling around the den. At breakfast the next morning Janina confronted him.

"Look, David. If this spray does turn out to be something lethal, what are we going to do about it?"

"Take it to the authorities, I suppose."

"We already said that the company owns the town. The police are on Langtree's side, too. How about if we take it to the public? I know a reporter who works for the *Evening Sentinel*. I helped him out of a spot when his daughter was in the hospital. If we can get the proof to him, I'm sure he'll print it."

"You might have an idea there. Are you sure you can get him to listen?"

"Once we get the results of the analysis, I'll make him listen if I have to tie him down," she said reaching for the phone book.

It was less than an hour later when David's chemist friend called with the results they expected. The insecticide was not malathion at all but a new chemical compound that none of them had heard of. As to its toxicity, the results so far were questionable. Janina and David agreed it was time to call the press.

Maxwell Bosch looked like his name; short, stocky, with thinning hair. If he had something of a cynical attitude, one could only blame it on the company he kept. Max covered Willowbrook's crime beat in addition to doing an occasional feature for the *Evening Sentinel*. He welcomed any leads he could get, but when he heard David and Janina's story, his eyebrows lifted.

"What we've got here is a story of major proportions, if what you say is true." He had been writing steadily for several minutes when he stopped and wiped a chubby hand across his shaggy beard. This could blow the top off Langtree Labs, not to mention city hall. I wonder who else is involved. The feds, maybe?"

David shrugged. "I doubt it. There's certainly no indication of it, but it's not impossible. It just doesn't seem quite professional enough for that. Somebody is determined to hide something, though."

"Too true, buddy. But right now everything hinges on whether or not this new spray is toxic. Who'd you say ran the tests?"

"I didn't and I won't, but I can give you a small sample of the insecticide."

His smile was bland, but Janina detected a hidden intensity. "Can't blame a guy for trying, old buddy. The next thing is, are you and Janina going to give me trouble about using your names?"

Janina tensed. "Do you have to?"

Max shook his head. "We could run it blind, but it's bound to lose a lot of punch. Not much credibility in that kind of story. Just something to wrap the garbage in."

She looked up at David and he nodded. Janina resigned herself to the unwanted publicity. "All right, Max. I suppose I knew this was going to happen when I called you. But tone down our involvement as much as you can, will you?"

"I'll do my best for you, Janina. You sure helped us out when Katy needed those pints of AB negative blood."

David handed him a small bottle containing a sample of the new chemical. "Be careful with this, Max. Don't get it on your skin and don't inhale it. I can't vouch for its safety."

"Will do. Thanks, old man. My boss can get this analyzed in a hurry. I think we've got us a story here."

"Will you call me either here or at the hospital and let me know?" Janina asked.

"As soon as I get a verdict from upstairs. Sometime before dinner, I hope."

David put his arm around Janina's shoulder as they walked Max to the door. It was going to be a long day.

THE MORNING SEEMED ENDLESS despite the flood of appointments Janina had scheduled. It was the day Ms Bonner's fifth-grade class was to tour the hospital and that took nearly two hours. Janina left messages to be notified immediately if Max or David called, but after a couple dozen scattered phone calls before eleven, her phone remained silent. The waiting was nearly unbearable. Aside from that, she wanted to be with David.

She was beginning to think she was paranoid because she had the strangest feeling that she was the prime topic of conversation among her fellow workers. It wasn't so much that they avoided her. They just weren't as outgoing and friendly as they had always been. It was as if lines were being drawn between her and administration, and the nursing staff was afraid to take her side.

Casey, outspoken as usual, tried to give her some advice. "Listen, Jan. We all know you're incredibly brave to stand up for what you think is going on, but you make waves, you gotta take the chance of getting swamped. Am I right?"

"Of course you're right, but it doesn't help a darn bit."

"Sure, we all think it's strange that there are so many cases of pancreatitis, but if the spray had anything to do with it, you'd think somebody besides you would be crusading against it. I mean, there hasn't been anything in the papers or on TV. If we knew more about it, maybe more of us would stand behind you."

"Just keep watching the papers. Unless I'm wrong, this whole thing might break tonight."

Casey gave her a hug. "I sure hope so, for your sake."

Back in her office Janina checked her phone to make sure it was working. Finally, out of frustration, she called David. He answered on the first ring.

"Janina, what the devil is going on down there? I've been trying to phone you for a half-hour."

"You have? That's odd. I can't understand it, David. I've been here in the office for the last hour but my phone hasn't rung. What's up?"

"Max called. His editor refused to print the insecticide article."

Her frustration was quickly turning to anger. "But why? We certainly gave them enough proof."

"He said it was too inflammatory. It would serve no purpose to excite the public, and anyway, the situation is nearly under control."

Janina got up and began to pace the room. "Then the editor must know what's going on. And how come they're still spraying if the situation is under control?"

"Your guess is as good as mine. Listen, love. Haven't you had enough of this cloak-and-dagger business?"

"Have you? Do you want to quit?"

"We don't seem to be getting anywhere."

"This was supposed to be a vacation for you," she mused. "I guess it hasn't been much fun. My fault, too. I'm sorry I let you get involved."

"If you're involved, I'm involved. Jan, you must

know that by now." His voice came across the telephone line warm and loving. "Janina, I'm nothing without you. I care for you more than I could have believed possible."

She laced the telephone cord between her fingers, wanting desperately to believe him but afraid of the hurt that might destroy her this time if he left her again. David seemed to be hinting that he wanted her to stop trying to play Mata Hari. Heaven knew she wasn't winning any friends with her single-minded pursuit of the truth. She was tired of the whole business. She wanted to give it all up and go home and play house with David.

At that moment a slightly plump pink lady, with a face to match her dress, stuck her head in the door. "Ms Scott. Mr. Baker, the administrator, has been trying to get you but your line is busy. He'd like to see you upstairs in his office, STAT."

Janina waved a thank-you. "David. I'm sorry. I have to go. Randolph Baker has been trying to reach me. He wants to see me upstairs."

"Trouble?"

"What else?"

"Hang in there, Jan. Don't let him bully you. There are plenty of jobs for people with your training. You can come to work for me whenever you want to." His voice softened. "I know that doesn't mean much to you right now, but I want you to know I'll be there when you need me. Damn. I feel so helpless. I want to be there with you."

His words gave her a warm glow. "I wish you were here, too, David."

"I could be in a matter of minutes."

"No. This is something I have to do myself, but I

appreciate your support. Just knowing that you are on my side makes me feel better about this whole thing." She was tempted to change her mind at the last minute but she reminded herself that it was important to stand on her own feet. "Thanks, David. I'd better go now." She gently put the receiver back on the cradle and began to fix her hair and face. There was no doubt in her mind that she was going to need the added self-confidence it gave her.

By the time she reached the administrative suite she felt almost jubilant. David had succeeded in convincing her of his sincerity. She loved him and she wanted him for as long as she could have him, be it a day, a month or a lifetime. If Baker got too tough, she'd simply hand him her resignation and tell him what he could do with it. They needed her more than she needed them.

She was smiling when he rose to greet her, but there was no friendliness in the look he returned. "Sit down, Janina. I'll make this short and to the point. As of noon today you have been indefinitely suspended from work here at the hospital. Your actions are unconscionable, as is your lack of respect for authority." He smoothed his hand over the front of his vest in a self-satisfied gesture. "Mr. Guilford will take over your office until we see fit to reinstate you."

She felt as if she had been hit in the chest with a lead pipe. "I don't understand, Randolph. Just what do you mean? I have never challenged your authority."

"This business with the newspaper is the last straw. You've meddled enough. I have the board's permission to take appropriate action, and you must consider yourself on disciplinary suspension until further notice."

Janina rose. "Is there anything else?" He didn't bother to answer and she turned and walked out, closing the door softly behind her. Her knees had turned to water before she reached the elevator. Fortunately there was a bench next to the wall and she sat down slowly as if her very bones ached with the effort.

"Damn, damn, damn," she whispered under her breath. Suspension was the last thing she had expected. She was shocked to the core and it apparently showed on her face. Maxine Lowden, the tall, svelte day-shift head nurse from the obstetrics ward, met her in the hall.

"Janina, what happened to you? You look like one of the patients instead of staff."

Janina laughed humorlessly. "Right now, I'm neither. I've just been suspended from active duty until further notice."

"Because of the mess you started over the pancreatitis cases?"

"Yup. Randolph Baker ordered me to close my office and lock it up."

"I can't believe it." She stabbed her black chignon with the pencil she had been carrying. "But what can you do about it? You aren't going to let that vanilla-pudding dictator get away with it, are you?"

"I don't have much choice at the moment, but I'll be back on staff if I have to go to the federal inspector."

Maxine's voice dropped to a whisper. "Is it true that you think the fruit-fly spray is behind the pancreatitis?"

Janina looked at her in surprise. "Where did you hear that?"

"Huh? I dunno." Maxine shifted uneasily. "You know how those things get around."

"Well, at this point I can tell you one thing for sure.

They aren't using malathion to spray for the fruit fly. You take a good smell next time the helicopters go over. It doesn't smell like kerosene, the way it did when we had the Medfly invasion. This spray stinks like rotten licorice.''

Maxine's eyes widened. "I don't understand how you do it, Janina. You seem to know everything that's going on. I never even think of things like that, let alone have the courage to do something about it."

Janina grimaced as they continued down the hallway. "Sure, Maxine. Terrific. Look where it got me. Suspended."

WORD HAD APPARENTLY GOTTEN AROUND that she was in trouble. Only a few people dared offer a word of encouragement. She could have done without it. The numbness was beginning to wear off and it hurt too damn much. Right now the only person she wanted to see was David.

He nearly hit the ceiling when she finally got home and told him what happened. "I'm tempted to go up there and punch the bastard out. Come here, Janina." He held open his arms to her and she didn't have to be asked twice. Only with David could she let down her emotional barriers and cry.

"It...it's the first time anyone has ever talked like that to me," she sobbed. "Suspended until further notice. What am I going to do, David?" She rested her head against his chest, inhaling the comfort of his familiar scent, feeling the steady beat of his heart against her cheek.

He held her and rubbed her back as he buried his face in her hair. "Don't think about it right now. The time will go fast and before you're ready for it, they'll be calling you back to work."

"I'm glad you're here."

"So am I, love. So am I."

His breath feathered the hair at the back of her neck and she snuggled closer, running her hands beneath his jacket, glorying in the warmth of his body, the solid strength in his muscles. His fingers gently kneaded her back, stroking, teasing until she relaxed against him. He touched her forehead with his lips, content for the moment to be there for her when she needed him.

Reaching up, she cupped the back of his head in her hand and, pulling his face down to hers, kissed him softly on the mouth. "Thank you. I'm all right now. It just seemed like everything dumped on me at once."

She moved away, rubbing her elbows in concentration. "I just had a thought, David. Mr. Baker mentioned something about my creating trouble with the press. How could he know about it already? It was only this morning that Max went to his editor."

"The editor must have called Randolph Baker right after he talked to Max. It sounds like there's a definite connection among all of the local people who have any degree of influence in the community."

"Damn! I hate politics. I wish I'd never gotten mixed up in it. I've had it. I refuse to even think about the malathion thing anymore."

David apparently was not listening. Suddenly he smacked his forehead with his hand. "Well, I'll be damned. Now I know where I saw Randolph Baker before. He was one of the blue suits I saw through the open doorway at the meeting at city hall."

Janina whirled around. "My God, that must mean that Baker is in this even deeper than I thought."

"Sure." David's tone was dry. "That information and fifty cents will buy you a cup of coffee." He shoved his hands into his pockets and stared into the fish tank. "It looks pretty hopeless to me. We've done all we can, Janina. We might as well let it go."

"I hate letting them get away with it."

"Let's try not to think about it. Now that you're a lady of leisure, what say we plan something fun for tomorrow? You can help me celebrate my vacation."

"And mine," she added dryly. She really wasn't in the mood to plan a celebration, but out of fairness to David, she agreed.

He was as excited as a little boy. "I was thinking we could take a drive down to Santa Cruz and check out the boardwalk, then come back past the begonia gardens."

Her face lit up. "You don't have to do that for me, David. I know you aren't all that crazy about plants."

"We could even stop for a late lunch at Big Basin Park. It isn't as fast as Route 17 but it's more interesting. Or maybe you don't want to go."

She laughed. "You know me better than that. I hate to wait until tomorrow, but I'll do the laundry tonight and make the time go faster."

THEY GOT AN EARLY START the next morning and ate a late breakfast at an oceanside restaurant in Santa Cruz. When the stores opened they did a little window shopping then walked along the boardwalk and watched the children ride the merry-go-round and roller coaster. Janina hadn't mentioned the begonia gardens, but David didn't forget. They spent nearly two hours touring the exciting Antonelli Nursery, with its vast displays of dazzling foliage plants. David bought a magnificent rex begonia specimen called Pink Champagne, which fairly crackled with brilliant shadings of color from pale pink to magenta to bluish-white.

"This should look magnificent in the corner of your patio where the sunlight is indirect."

Janina shot a look at him. "Pretty good. I'll make a gardener of you yet."

He nodded. "If that's what it takes."

By the time they reached Big Basin Park, Janina and David were starved. They had bought enough take-out fried chicken and fresh fruit to feed a half-dozen people. David drove along the meandering roads until they came to a secluded table beneath a canopy of enormous redwood trees. The ground was thickly carpeted with dried needles that absorbed the sounds of their intrusion into the forest and gave off a pungent odor of pine.

Janina breathed deeply and let the solitude flow through her. "This is heaven, isn't it?"

"Remember the last time we had fried chicken?" His wraparound grin went all the way up to his eyes.

"How could I forget? You fed most of it to the crabs, David."

"Um. That was the year they nearly became extinct."

"Strictly a rumor, but I know a certain doctor who is fast becoming an endangered species." She brushed needles from the picnic table. "Can we eat first, then go for a walk?"

"Sure, but I think we have company."

Janina looked around and saw two adult deer and two fawns, their spots already fading to a soft brown, standing not forty feet away. She caught her breath in wonder. "They're not the least bit afraid. Throw me an apple, David. I want to see if they'll come up to us."

As they stood there together, the deer came toward

them, stopping now and again to test the air. The doe was the boldest of the group. Her wet muzzle nudged the apple from Janina's hand and moments later, the other three came to get their share.

David opened the bag that held the bucket of fried chicken. One of the deer sniffed a piece and turned away in disgust. Shortly afterward all four of them took off at a trot in the direction of the woods.

Janina laughed. "And all this time you teased me because nobody wanted *my* chicken. Has it occurred to you that we always end up feeding the animals?"

"Well, this is one animal that could eat even your cooking right at this moment. I bought some sodas, too, in case you're thirsty."

They ate slowly, savoring their closeness and the treat of being out-of-doors in the sunshine. Afterward they walked one of the trails that skirted a stream and picked up colored pebbles, bright and icy-cold from the water. When they came to a playground, Janina found a tire suspended from a tree by a long rope and sat in it while David swung her high in the air. She leaned back, letting her head hang down.

"This is fun. I haven't felt this young for the past five years."

He caught her as she swung toward him and slipped from the swing into his arms. Holding her there, feeling free, her feet off the ground, her eyes bright with excitement, David yearned for her with a longing that threatened to choke him. What was it about her that got into the very pores of his being? It went beyond the mere physical. She was pretty in every sense of the word, but it was some inner quality that made his heart ache for the want of her. She had enthusiasm, a glow of excitement that radiated into those around

her. Life without her would be like living in a darkened
room.

Janina wondered what he was thinking as he held
her. His eyes seemed to memorize her face...as if...
Oh God, don't let him leave me again, she prayed
silently.

Slowly she slid down until her toes touched the
ground and her mouth met his. She kissed him warmly, and there was no touch of the child in her kiss. She
was all woman.

After a while they wandered farther upstream and
watched the ducks, and the children throwing scraps
of bread. Janina caught David watching a blue-eyed,
elfin little girl who kept trying to feed a duck that had
only one leg. The other ducks kept crowding in, but
the little girl was determined and kept shooing the
others away until her duck ate his fill.

"What are you thinking, David?" Janina asked.

"That little girl. If we had a child, she might look
like her. Do you want children, Janina, or is your
career more important?"

Janina laughed, taken aback. "You ask about my
career on the day I'm practically fired? Seriously,
though? I want everything...children, a career of
sorts, hobbies, cats, a chance to travel. In short, the
good life. Just like any other normal American."

"You didn't say anything about a husband."

"So I didn't."

"You plan to be a single mother, then?"

Janina grinned. "No. I'm old-fashioned enough to
believe in the complete family unit. I told you, I want
everything."

"I'm awfully glad to hear that."

She looked at him quizzically. It seemed natural to

ask him what he wanted from life, but something held her back. Maybe she was afraid to know what he really wanted, now that he was a free man and a wealthy one to boot.

As she stepped up on the bridge that crossed the creek, David turned her toward him, placing his hands on the wooden railing behind her. He kissed her softly on the tip of her nose.

"I want what you want, Janina. No matter what it is."

The little girl laughed as she watched them and David and Janina laughed back.

After they returned to her condominium, they went for a swim in the nearly deserted pool. It was a Tahoe night. Most of the young and unattached had opted for the chartered bus ride up to the casinos.

Janina floated on her back as she watched the blinking lights of small planes against the backdrop of stars in the velvet sky. It was so peaceful. When David finished his thirty laps, they stretched out on lounge chairs at the far end of the pool. It had been a full day and they were tired, but pleasantly so. David talked for a long time about the clinic he wanted to build in San Diego for low-income families. He didn't say so, but Janina suspected it was his way of giving back some of the blessings that had come his way. Although he rarely went to church, David had a strong Christian background. She liked that. It made her feel closer to him.

They stayed by the pool until the night air became too cold, then they went inside to shower and to change clothes.

The telephone had been ringing insistently for several minutes when Janina dashed into the den with a towel wrapped around her middle.

"Why didn't you answer it, David?"

"I didn't want to embarrass you."

"Oh. . ." She shrugged as she picked up the receiver and said, "Hello."

"Janina, it's Deb. Listen, I don't have time to talk. I'm at the hospital with Doug. His father is awful sick and I thought maybe, since you work here, you could come down and—"

"What's wrong with him, Debbie?"

"Gosh, it's. . .just a minute, Doug says that it's his dad's pancreas. He's not too good, Janina. They have him in the emergency room now. We brought him here to Mercy so that Doug would be able to visit him between school and work." She paused to catch her breath. "Could you come over, Jan? Doug's holding up all right, but I know he'd feel better if you were here."

"I'll be right there, Debbie. Take care of Doug."

Janina left the bedroom door open while she got dressed and explained the situation to David, who insisted on going with her. She would have hesitated to ask him, but having David along was just the emotional support she needed.

It seemed to take forever to get there. The traffic along Sutter Street was bumper to bumper because of the grand opening of a new shopping center. David made a sharp left turn and drove through an alley to Camino where there were more traffic lights but fewer cars.

Janina had been moving restlessly when she finally spoke. "David, I was just thinking. Doug and his father live way outside of town, toward Fremont. If he has pancreatitis, how did he manage to get it? The spray planes haven't been covering that area this time."

"Good question. Maybe he ate some fruit that had been sprayed."

"I guess it's possible."

He reached over and rested his hand on her thigh. "I thought you had put all those questions out of your mind for the duration." There was no criticism in his comment, but it was obvious to Janina that he was concerned.

She stroked his hand with her fingertips. "I wish I could. It isn't easy. It's like having a splinter in your hand that's buried too deeply to get out, but whenever something brushes against it, you feel the twinge. You know it's there, but you can't do anything about it."

"And if you don't get it out, you know it's going to get infected."

"Exactly." She straightened as he made the turn into the parking lot. "My parking space is down the second aisle from the entrance. Not as close as the doctors' reserved spaces, but it beats looking for a place to park."

"The place is jammed. I hope they allow for another parking lot when they finish the new wing."

Debbie and Doug sat close together on a wicker sofa in the ER waiting room, which was empty except for a young woman with a sleepy-looking little boy. Janina's heart warmed as she saw Doug, his sandy-blond hair tousled from running his fingers through it. He was taller than Debbie by a few inches, a little too thin, but his heavy schedule probably accounted for that. They both wore jeans and cotton shirts, and they looked terribly young and vulnerable as they held hands and talked quietly.

When Debbie spotted her, she jumped up and threw

her arms around Janina. "Hey, you guys. Thanks for coming." Her voice sounded relieved.

After David and Doug were introduced, David and Janina went in to see Mr. Fairfax, but he was so uncomfortable that they didn't stay long, nor did they try to question him.

"What do you think, David?" Janina asked when they were alone for a minute.

He shrugged. "Hard to tell without an examination. He has all the visual symptoms of hemorrhagic pancreatitis, but I can't tell if he's approaching the critical stage. They'll be taking him down to OR shortly, I suspect."

Janina recognized the nurse on duty, a special friend of the administrator. Common sense told her to avoid making any more waves if she ever hoped to be taken off suspension, but she asked anyway.

The nurse was cool to the point of frostbite. "I'm sorry, Ms Scott, but as you know, all questions must be directed to the attending physician and those only from the immediate family."

"Thank you, Mrs. Fredricks. I certainly appreciate your thoughtfulness," Janina said with undue warmth.

David looked surprised. "How could you be so nice to her? She was a first-class jerk."

Janina grinned. "Kill 'em with kindness. It gets to them every time."

When they got back to the waiting room, Doug and Debbie were alone. Debbie had her arm around Doug's shoulder and she was obviously trying to comfort him. Janina felt good about it. Doug was crazy about Debbie, and Debbie, in her own way, was attracted to Doug. He was good for her. If she would only accept the fact that his commitment to his career had to come first.

"How does he look to you, Dr. Madison?" Doug asked.

"Make it David. I was just telling Janina that it's hard to tell without doing an examination, but he seems to be holding his own. They'll probably be taking him down to Surgery, but with your training, I'm sure you expected that."

He nodded. "It's going to be a long recovery, isn't it?"

"I'm afraid so. But he has a lot going for him, basic good health. You have every reason to be encouraged."

"It's going to drive him up the wall, though. Dad's used to working hard. He just got a big contract a week or so ago, and I doubt if it's finished; he was doing it alone. The guy who works with him is off somewhere on his honeymoon."

"Well, it's a funny thing about recuperation. Most people can handle it pretty well. Especially if they've been sick enough that they have to undergo surgery."

"But what could've caused it? My dad's tough, you know? He never gets sick."

"Does he drink very much?"

"Dad? Gosh no. He doesn't have more than a half-dozen beers a month. Now that Mom is dead, all he lives for is his work and the day when I graduate from med school. He owns a small air-conditioning company that puts in heating and cooling systems for stores and places like that."

Janina looped her arm over the back of her chair. "Has anyone else in his family ever had pancreatitis, as far as you know?"

"No. I looked it up in my medical dictionary and I

couldn't find a thing in my dad's history that would point to a tendency to be receptive to the disease."

David leaned forward, resting his elbows on his knees, his chin on his hands. "Do you know if your father has been working with fruit trees or out in his yard lately?"

"I can answer that one easy. Dad hates working outside. Our whole yard is covered with lava rock and redwood bark so he doesn't even have to cut grass. Why? Would that have meant something?"

David shrugged. "Just a thought."

Debbie stirred restlessly. "Jan, do you think maybe you could use your influence and speed things up a little? Doug and I have been waiting for a long time for the results of the tests."

Janina sighed, glancing quickly at David and then back. "Sorry, Deb. I don't think I'd be much help. Anyway, it looks like Mr. Fairfax is getting the best of care." Janina was grateful that David didn't say anything about the fact that she had been suspended. Not that she felt guilty about it. She did what she had to do. If the hospital chose to discipline her for it, that was their decision. No point, though, in burdening her sister with the problem.

Then, too, it was a question of pride. She felt a responsibility to set some kind of example for Debbie. Janina was always the steady one; she never got into trouble, never did anything to upset anyone. It hurt to be reprimanded. It would have hurt doubly to have the family find out about it.

While they were waiting for the doctor, they heard the helicopters fly over the hospital, and the sound, though muted, was ominous. Debbie and a group of visitors who had just come in went to the window to watch. The copters were not actually spraying at the time but were on a return flight to the staging area. Janina thought about what she and David had done the night before and it seemed more like part of a dream until David looked over at her and grinned.

Chapter Eight

A short time later, Dr. Jameson came in to talk to Doug. David had worked with him years ago, and the two men were able to discuss the case in private. Afterward, David reassured Doug that his father's condition, though serious, was not critical. They elected to wait until the following morning to take him to Surgery, allowing time for his condition to stabilize.

Mr. Fairfax, over Doug's protests, insisted that his son go home and try to get some sleep. Debbie asked if she could spend the night with Janina instead of driving back to Castro Valley. Before she remembered that David was staying with her, Janina agreed.

Debbie didn't seem the least bit surprised to find out that David had moved in with Janina, and she acted amazed when Janina told her that she was going to share Janina's bedroom.

"Look, you guys," she said with a superior little smile. "David doesn't have to move out of your bedroom just because I'm here. I can sleep in the den."

Janina's face turned red. "David has been using the den. You can share my bedroom." She carefully avoided looking at David. If he made some smart remark now, she'd never forgive him.

Debbie turned her back to David and drew a square with her fingers. Janina was fuming, but she kept her mouth shut, knowing that to argue with Debbie would only make things worse.

The two women talked for a while after they went to bed. Debbie admitted that she had been to a party last weekend with Johnny Espinosa, but they both had too much to drink and she had decided to cool it for a while and start seeing Doug. She had been at Doug's house, listening to records when his father started getting quite sick.

"I'm glad you were there with Doug when he needed you," Janina said.

Debbie shrugged and rolled over. "I didn't do anything. I was just there, that's all."

"Sometimes, that's all that's necessary. It's good to have someone to talk to."

"Like you and David?"

"I guess."

"Except he wants to do more than talk."

"Come on, Debbie. Right now David and I are just friends."

"There's no such thing as 'just friends' between a man and a woman. All the time you're with a man there's always that little undercurrent of sex. David's different, I'll admit, but if you don't give him some encouragement, he's gonna split."

"Even if I do encourage him, he might leave me. He did before."

"So? If he does, that's life. Nobody gets a guarantee on happiness. David's a terrific guy. You're really crazy if you let him get away this time."

Janina looked up at the ceiling, watching the flash of headlights as cars turned the corner at Palmdale Drive. "Maybe I don't have any choice, Deb."

"That's dumb. It's plain to see the guy's in love with you."

"Like Doug is with you?"

"That's no big secret. I just don't know if I can wait until he's ready for marriage."

"You're young for marriage, Deb. It wouldn't seem so long if you were going to school or working at a steady job."

Debbie sighed. "I don't want to think about it."

Janina smiled as she turned over and tucked her hand beneath her cheek. When Debbie said she didn't want to think about it, Janina knew from experience that that was exactly what she was doing. She wanted to hug her sister, but it wasn't the right moment.

As it turned out, the next morning Janina had to tell Debbie that she had been suspended; she could think of no other reason for not going to work. She did manage to gloss over the reason, and simply attributed it to a policy disagreement. Debbie was properly indignant, but concern for Doug and his father soon replaced it. Janina breathed easier when she got through the explanation without having to mention the malathion business.

When they arrived at the hospital, the man who had taken over her office had also taken over her parking space. "Damn!" she said, her face getting red. "Freddie Guilford has been trying to move in on my job for over a year. Boy, would I love to let all the air out of his tires."

David seemed amused by her short burst of temper. "Maybe we should hire a hit man." Janina gave him a look that would have withered an ordinary man.

They met Doug in the lobby and the four of them went up to see Mr. Fairfax as he was being prepped for surgery.

Janina was conscious of the occasional quickly averted looks she received from some of the hospital personnel, people who she thought were her friends. A few people had the courage to come up to her and tell her how much she was missed and how hard it was to get along with Freddie Guilford. It wasn't a small thing for them to do. Nothing passed word more quickly than the hospital grapevine, and sides were quickly drawn when it came to keeping one's job.

Janina was grateful for the encouragement. She would have liked to have gotten some papers from her desk, but it wasn't worth the risk of running into Guilford. Her records were in good order. If he needed any help, he could ask for it.

David was gone for a while. Janina was curious but didn't think of asking him where he had been. When the noon hour came a short time later, David invited the three of them to have lunch at a local restaurant. As they were leaving the parking lot, David slowed down as he passed Janina's assigned slot.

"Would you look at that?" he murmured. "That car has two flat tires. Good thing you didn't park there, Jan."

Janina was appalled. "David, you didn't!"

"Who me? You know me better than that, Janina."

"I thought I did but I'm beginning to see a new side of you, Dr. Madison."

Debbie let out a whoop. "Come on, Jan. You've got to be kidding. David is too straight to do anything illegal."

David looked around with an expression of angelic innocence. "I'm glad somebody respects me."

Janina chewed her lip to keep from laughing. If only Debbie could have seen them on their commando raid.

But she wouldn't have believed it, even if she had seen it with her own eyes.

Mr. Fairfax came through his surgery with remarkable ease. Doug and Debbie spent the rest of the day at the hospital. Janine and David left as soon as they knew that Mr. Fairfax's condition was stable.

"So what do you want to do now?" David asked.

"Get as far away from the hospital as possible."

"I don't think my passport is in order."

"David, be serious. I ought to go home and clean house now that I have all this free time on my hands. I've been thinking about painting my bedroom, but I never have enough time when I'm working."

"I could help you. Of course, the paint fumes would drive you out and you'd have to sleep somewhere else tonight."

"Hm. Like the den, for instance?"

"The thought crossed my mind."

"I didn't think about the paint smell."

"Me and my big mouth." David grinned.

"Well, it would have gotten a bit crowded, wouldn't it? With the three of us, I mean. Debbie will no doubt sleep over again."

"Obstacles. I keep running into brick walls. Am I doing something wrong?"

Janina's face softened. "No, doctor. Your bedside manner is above reproach. It's those brilliant ideas you'd better watch. Good heavens. I hate to think what would have happened if someone had seen you letting the air out of Freddie Guilford's tires." She smiled, delighted with David's shameless prank, which was performed, of course, on her behalf. "It served Freddie right. He had a habit of cozying up to administration in order to secure his career advancement."

"I admit nothing." David reached across the seat for her hand. "Speaking of bedside manner, Janina. We have the whole afternoon to ourselves. I wouldn't object to spending it in your bedroom."

She looked over at him, and for a moment their gazes met. He looked tender and sweet and vulnerable. She knew David. He was warm-blooded, virile. It wasn't like him to leash that splendid passion, but he was giving her a chance to come to terms with herself. While he was patient and understanding, she was being less than fair to him. But was she ready to take the chance again?

His steady gaze questioned her and she didn't know the answer. Tears welled up behind her eyes. "David. I want to, you must know that, but I just can't let go."

He squeezed her hand, then patted her knee. "We belong together and I think you know it deep down."

She wanted to believe it. She wanted *him* to believe it, not just in the heat of the moment, but in the cold light of day when her hair was a mess and the dishes weren't done and there was cat hair all over the rug.

David made a left turn when the green arrow came on, and headed toward her condominium. Every day he spent with Janina, the thought of leaving her became a little more difficult. At the same time, it became increasingly hard to maintain his distance. The day was fast approaching when one of them would have to make a decision.

WHEN THEY ARRIVED HOME, Cinnamon came toward them, taking time along the way to stretch her back. David scratched her chin and she purred loud enough to rattle the shutters.

"All right, David. Quit trying to woo my cat away

from me. You've already got my mother and sister on your side.''

With one lazy motion he stood up, looped his arm around Janina's waist and pulled her against him. ''Maybe that's my trouble. I haven't been concentrating my energies on you. Did it occur to you that the house seemed very crowded with Debbie here last night? Don't get me wrong. I'd love to have her come to visit us, but not until a good long time after we're married.''

Janina tried to keep her voice from shaking. ''You're taking an awful lot for granted, Dr. Madison.''

''I take nothing for granted, but I'm trying to think positive. I lost you once before, Jan. I don't intend for that to happen again.'' He caught her wrists in one hand and pinned them behind her back.

''Sometimes I think the cavemen had the right idea in capturing their women and dragging them off to their caves. It sure saved a lot of time and misunderstandings.''

She studied him with a humorous glint in her eyes as she freed her hand. ''Don't tell me that after all this time you like your women to be passive. I didn't think you had changed that much. I seem to recall that whenever I did this, and this—'' she said, running her fingers lightly inside his shirt ''—that you always turned to a quivering mass of jelly.''

His eyes darkened to cobalt-blue. ''And you have learned to live dangerously, love. I'd advise you to put on your running shoes if you aren't ready to be carried off to bed.''

He kissed her before she could answer. It was just as well, because she was at a loss for words. David was becoming harder to resist with each passing day. He held her close in his arms as his chin dusted the top of her head. Her arms were around him and a tremulousness began to build inside her until she longed for him to forget her hesitation and take her to bed. But she couldn't bring herself to say the words.

His lips brushed her forehead and she closed her eyes in an agony of desire. When he spoke, his voice was thick with emotion.

"You'd love San Diego, Janina. I have a big beautiful home on the ocean. Lots of windows, a quarter-mile of private beach, a naturalized pool set among big old oak trees. There isn't anything I can't give you if you want it. We can travel, I'll build a greenhouse for all your growing things, and you won't even have to boil water for tea if you don't want to."

Something inside Janina began to curl up and wither as David continued to tell her about the pleasures he wanted to lavish upon her. She pulled away, but even before she did, David sensed that something was bothering her.

His voice was anxious. "What's wrong? What did I say, love?" He stroked her arm.

Janina shook her head. Her voice nearly choked in her throat. "Just stop it. I don't want to hear any more." She jumped up and ran into the kitchen.

David followed. "Dammit, Janina. You owe me an explanation. I don't deserve to be treated like that. One minute, you send off signals that make me think you can't wait for me to get you into bed. The next minute, you act as if you can't wait for me to leave." He got up and began to pace the floor.

Cinnamon flattened her ears and ran for safety beneath the kitchen table, but Janina couldn't escape so easily. She didn't want to say anything that would make

David leave. If he left now, she might never see him again. At the same time, she couldn't bear to have him touch her. She propped her hands behind her on the counter and faced him.

"Damn you, David. Do you think I want you to hand over Susan's possessions to me as if I were some kind of vulture waiting to rob her grave? Susan's house and Susan's beach, and Susan's swimming pool and don't forget Susan's money, of course." She ticked them off on her fingers, one by one. "Tell me, David, aren't there any jewels?"

His eyes were blazing. "As a matter of fact, there are quite a number of them. What is it, Janina? Are you jealous of her? My God, she's dead and buried. Susan can't hurt you now."

"But she does, whenever I think about the years we wasted. She'll always be there between us every time we make love on her bed, in her house, under her damned oak trees."

"You're acting like a child. What the devil do you want me to do? Give everything away? If that's what you want, Janina, I'll do it."

"Now who's acting childish? Just leave me alone, David. I don't want to talk to you right now."

"My sentiments exactly," he said, turning and striding quickly toward the den.

Janina stood there watching him until he closed the door. She was too numb to stop him, too distraught to do anything except grasp the edge of the countertop until her fingers burned with pain. But it was nothing compared to the pain in her chest. She was filled to the bursting point with the hurt that had grown like a poisonous weed inside her.

Why couldn't he understand that it was Susan who

had destroyed them three years ago? Susan the weak, the dependent. Why was it that the weak so often came out the winners by the sheer fact of their existence? Knowing that Susan was dead didn't make it any easier. Alive, Janina could have fought her, but even in her death Susan had the power to make Janina feel selfish.

She wanted to cry, but the tears wouldn't come. It was their first real fight. When David left her for Susan, they had chosen their words carefully, avoiding the subtle cruelties that so often go with broken relationships. Now she didn't know if there would ever be another chance for them. She longed to go to him, do anything, promise anything, before the breach could become permanent, but she held back.

Cinnamon crawled out from under the table and warily headed toward the patio chow line, as David called her food and water bowls. An irritated meow left no doubt that it was empty. Janina sighed and went to the refrigerator to get the rest of the can of Little Friskies.

It was then that she remembered that she had invited Debbie and Doug to come for dinner. Normally it would have been a small thing. She could have started early to prepare the food in the hope that everything would be edible. Or as a last resort, she could have gone to the deli for take-out food, but now the thought of preparing a meal was the last straw. She burst into tears and sat down at the table, burying her head in her hands.

David found her there a few minutes later, eyes red, hair rumpled as if she had just crawled out of bed. He felt something twist inside of him and he yearned to comfort her.

"Janina," he whispered, rubbing her back, then

bending down to kiss the nape of her neck. "Don't cry, love. We'll work it out. Can't you believe that?"

She nodded. "I want to. I hope we can, David."

He cupped her elbows in his hands and lifted her until she stood facing him. "Then stop crying and let's do something fun."

"I can't. I forgot that I invited Debbie and Doug for dinner. I knew they wouldn't feel like going to a restaurant."

"Oh, God. Is that all? I'll run over to the market for steaks and broil them on the gas grill. We can have salad and some fresh rolls and maybe peaches or melon for dessert. Okay?"

Her eyelashes were beaded with tears and she blinked rapidly. "You don't mind?"

He kissed the tip of her nose. "Feed the cat while I'm gone."

It seemed as if a gigantic weight had been lifted from her chest. Janina prided herself on being capable, self-sufficient, even if she couldn't cook, and it struck her that she had overreacted to a perfectly ordinary situation. But how wonderful it felt to have David there to look after things when she needed him.

Then she thought of Susan, who had been dying when David married her. "Oh, God," Janina whispered, and the words were torn from the depths of her soul. "Poor Susan. How much she must have needed him. No wonder he couldn't say no to her."

Janina stroked Cinnamon's back as the cat, belly close to the floor, sneaked up on the bowl of food to test the scent. *If someone I cared for needed me, wouldn't I have made the same decision?* Janina asked herself. She knew the answer without having to pause to weigh the options. As a nurse, she had been trained to put duty first, and before that, her parents had taught her a sense of obligation to do the right thing. David had similar values. It was one of the things she cherished about him. In all honesty, there was no way she could blame him for what he did.

Cinnamon took a tentative lick at the food, then turned around and gave Janina an affectionate nip.

ALTHOUGH JANINA OFFERED TO HELP DAVID with the dinner, he shooed her out of the kitchen once she had the table set on the patio, and she took the opportunity to shower and put on a nubby ivory dress that caressed her figure like liquid silk. She took extra time to blow-dry her hair, and it fluffed around her face in soft, shining waves of golden brown. Her sandals were the same brilliant turquoise as the Egyptian beadwork collar she wore around her neck.

It wasn't mere accident that the place mats and napkins matched her outfit. She loved turquoise and she especially liked the combination of ivory plates against the vivid background.

David had tried to buy flowers, but it was late in the day and there had been little to choose from. While he prepared the salad, Janina went into the scrap of garden that bordered her house and cut orange and yellow nasturtiums to fill an ivory pottery bowl. The effect was charming.

Just before Debbie and Doug were due to arrive, David changed into an ivory shirt and pale-blue pants that, when the light hit them just right, seemed to have a turquoise cast.

Debbie grinned when they opened the front door. "You two look like something from a Barbie Doll display. I like your his and hers outfits."

"Purely accidental," Janina said.

David grinned at Doug. "She's happy in her ignorance."

"I just talked to the hospital," Janina said, "and things are pretty quiet. They said your father is doing exceptionally well, Doug."

"He had a sip of water and doesn't have any pain, so far. He's already back in his room, so I guess the worst is over."

Debbie laced her fingers with Doug's. "I'm going up to sit with Mr. Fairfax tomorrow while Doug is in school."

"That's great," Janina said. She was delighted at the effect Doug was having on Debbie. Gone was her air of defiance, her acid wit that could easily scald. Whenever she thought no one was watching her, she looked at Doug as if she couldn't get enough of him. Oddly, there was a protective air about her where Doug was concerned, and it pleased Janina.

Doug covered Debbie's fingers with his other hand. "Dad's crazy about Debbie. Nobody else listens to all the stories he has to tell about his air-conditioning business. She'll probably hear all about his latest job out at Langtree Laboratories."

Janina put her glass down with a clatter. "Did you say Langtree Labs? What was your father doing there?"

Doug looked surprised at her sudden interest. "Well...you know, he installs air-conditioning systems for commercial buildings. He had done some work for Langtree before, and they asked him to replace some special filters in the duct works."

Janina started to say something, but David shot her a warning look. He spoke before Janina had a chance.

"They seem to have expanded quite a bit since I lived here. Was your dad working on the administration building?"

"No, it's not new. He was working on the small building at the far end of the east wing. The New Products Lab, I think it's called."

David nodded. "Sounds like a big job for one man to tackle."

"Yeah, but Tony was off somewhere on his honeymoon and the company didn't want inexperienced men working on the project, so Dad had to go it alone. He said it was like working at Fort Knox." Doug settled back on the sofa and crossed his legs. "Dad said they had a lot of security at the labs, but you wouldn't believe what I had to go through when I went out there to talk to the man Dad works for."

"That bad, huh?" David mused.

"Worse. Anyway, I guess the job is far enough along that Dad doesn't have to worry about the contract. And let me tell you, that's a relief."

They talked on for another half-hour, then Doug and Debbie left to go up to the hospital to see Mr. Fairfax. They were hardly out the door when Janina nearly exploded.

"How could you sit there and carry on a normal conversation? My God, do you know what this means? It *has* to be the source of the infection. They're probably manufacturing the stuff right on the premises."

David nodded. "It looks that way. Still, I don't know, Jan. There could be another explanation, but for the life of me I can't put my finger on it. I just feel like there's something we're overlooking."

"Damn! I wish I'd thought to look at the name on those tanker trucks."

"There wasn't any. They were just marked Flammable Materials."

Janina shot a look at him. "You don't miss much. I wish I were as observant."

"You are. We just notice different things." He put his arm across her shoulders as they walked toward the kitchen. "Listen, Jan. I don't think we ought to stir up any more trouble."

"Even knowing what we do now? David, we haven't tried TV or radio. I admit we failed with the newspaper, but maybe we could go on TV and tell the whole country our story. If they are using a substitute for malathion here in Santa Clara County, it's logical that they'd use it in other areas." She turned toward him, her eyes bright with excitement. "Remember the program you used to do for cable TV?"

"'What to Do before the Doctor Comes.'" He smiled slowly, remembering the trauma of that fifteen-minute live call-in television show. "That's an experience I'd rather forget."

"But why? Everyone loved it."

"What they really loved was the people who called in with lewd comments about the title of the show. We nearly were cited by the FCC the day the hooker called in and started to give me a blow-by-blow description of what she would like to do before the doctor came."

Janina giggled despite the need to be serious. "Oh, David. You know what I mean. If you could get on TV again, it would solve our whole problem."

He shook his head. "You'd have to get prior approval from the program director. It would be terribly involved, not to mention the fact that they would never go along with it."

They walked into the den and stood looking down at

the neons as their bodies flashed vivid red and blue in the water. "You're letting your wishful thinking get in the way of logic, Janina. If the mayor and the head of the hospital and the newspaper editor are a part of the cover-up, you can just bet that the rest of the media have also been cautioned to keep this thing under wraps. The sensible thing to do is forget it."

"I wish I could, but I can't, David."

"Neither can I."

She went over to the stereo and pushed a cassette into the slot. The thunder and lightning sounds of "One Stormy Night" filled the room with an explosion of sensations. It fit her mood. She was frustrated both mentally and physically, and she wanted to crawl out of her skin and start afresh.

"Want to go for a swim, David? We have a little time before the spray planes come over. After that, they cover the pool."

"Sure. Might as well. I can use the exercise after that porterhouse I put away."

"I haven't thanked you for playing cook. You were superb, as always."

He looked at her and for one brief moment Janina thought he was going to try to seduce her, but the moment passed. He shook his head as if to clear it. "I'll meet you at the pool," he said. And there was no trace of warmth in his voice.

Janina suspected that she had somehow hurt his feelings. She hadn't intended to. For the rest of the evening, she tried to be careful of the things she said and did. More than once their bodies brushed against each other in the pool, but she kept things light and fun in order to avoid a misunderstanding. The swim helped burn off some of her nervous energy, and she managed to sleep better than she had for several days.

The next day Doug's father had improved considerably and he insisted that Doug and Debbie take the afternoon off to go to the beach. They invited Janina and David to go along, but Janina sensed that they wanted to be alone.

That left her alone with David with nothing to keep them occupied. Out of frustration and self-preservation, Janina began cleaning house. She started with the kitchen, emptying each cabinet, filling the dishwasher with dishes she hadn't used recently, washing the inside of the refrigerator with a vinegar solution.

By the time she got to the windows, David looked at her in speculation. "Janina. To what do we owe this sudden 'Little Suzy Homemaker' fit of enthusiasm? Your house was already immaculate."

She pushed the hair away from her face with the back of her hand. "It doesn't stay that way by itself, David."

"Oh, come on. You know very well that you're frustrated, and cleaning house is your method of working your way out of a situation. You forget, love, that I know you as well as I know myself."

He had analyzed her feelings correctly and it puzzled her that he understood her so well. She got down from the ladder and threw the towel onto the countertop. "Then why is it I don't know you that well?"

"Maybe you haven't tried."

"Maybe you're more secretive than I am."

"So what would you like to know?"

He looked so innocent, so eager, that she couldn't help laughing. "Oh, David. The things I'd like to know about you are things you'd never tell me. And if you did, I probably wouldn't believe you."

"You never know until you try, love." The mischief in his eyes put her on guard.

She shook her head. "No, my friend. Some things are better left to the imagination."

IT WAS NEARING TEN O'CLOCK that night when Doug brought Debbie home. Janina sensed immediately that something was wrong. Doug looked uneasy as Debbie barely took time to say hello before she headed toward the bedroom.

"What's wrong, Doug?" Janina asked in a tightly controlled voice. If Doug had hurt Debbie, she would never forgive him.

He looked first at Janina, then over to David and back. "I don't know what to do. Deb made me promise not to tell."

David stood up and all but grabbed Doug by the shirt. "Well, if you don't tell us pretty damn soon, I'm going to make you wish you had."

Janina put her hand on his arm. "David, please. If it's something we should know, Doug, then tell us, for heaven's sake."

"Debbie's going to kill me, but I think you should know. She got sick this afternoon. Her stomach. She thought it was a tuna salad sandwich that did it, but I don't know, Janina. I'm . . . well, I'm scared."

David had simmered down and assumed his professional demeanor. "When did she first get sick? What are her symptoms?"

"It started all of a sudden, about four o'clock. Epigastric abdominal pains—worse when she lies down—nausea, sweating."

A sliver of fear penetrated Janina's chest. "Had she been drinking?"

"Liquor, you mean? No. She just had an orange soda. I think she might have been drinking pretty heavily a couple days ago, though. She mentioned something about being hung over when I talked to her on the phone." He looked sideways. "I guess I shouldn't have told you that."

David swore softly. "Listen, Doug. This is not the time to play games. Did she mention any of these symptoms before today?"

"Not to me, she didn't." He fidgeted uncomfortably before he spoke. "I'm almost afraid to say this, but it sure sounds a lot like what my dad went through before I took him to the hospital." He wiped his hand across his mouth. "I know that the symptoms are common to a lot of other illnesses besides pancreatitis, but I just can't help but wonder—"

David interrupted. "I think maybe I'd better take a look at her, Janina. All right?"

Janina's face was numb with fear. She nodded.

Doug looked shaken. "I...I'm sorry, Janina. I feel so damn responsible. I know pancreatitis isn't communicable, but if Debbie has it, too, then—dammit. I love her, you know. I'd die before I'd let anything hurt her."

"I know, Doug. It's not your fault." She studied the back of her left hand, amazed that it should look unfamiliar, yet at the same time feeling completely detached from reality.

Doug continued as if unable to stop himself once he had decided to tell them the truth. "It happened so fast. One minute we were—were sitting on the sand, watching the gulls and stuff, the next minute she doubled over in pain."

He buried his head in his hands. "It's got to be just a stomachache. She couldn't have gotten pancreatitis just from being around my dad. Besides, if she caught it, I would have caught it, too. I practically carried him into the hospital that night.''

Janina pressed her fingertips together and held them to her face. Acute pancreatitis. The words haunted her like the clarion call of some ancient curse. Finally, she made up her mind. ''Doug, there's something I think you should know. David and I have been investigating the sudden increase in cases of acute pancreatitis. It's the reason I was suspended from the hospital staff.'' She cleared her throat, aware of the sensationalistic sound of what she was saying but committed to continue. ''I think there's some kind of cover-up taking place here in the city, perhaps even the whole county, but so far we can't make anyone listen.''

Doug's eyes were enormous. He swore softly as Janina continued. ''We know for a fact that the spray that's being used to control the fruit fly is not malathion, as we've been told. A friend of David's is trying to find out more about it, but he has to be careful. An awful lot of influential people seem to be involved.''

''I . . . this is like some kind of nightmare.''

''That's putting it mildly. Whatever you do, Doug, don't let this go any further. I wouldn't want Debbie to know.''

''You have my word on it. If I can be of any help, all you have to do is let me know what you want me to do.''

Janina gave him an affectionate hug. They were silent for several minutes. She knotted her fingers together. ''What can be taking so long in there?'' She got up and began to pace the floor. A few minutes later, David came out of the bedroom and put his arm around Janina's shoulder.

''Listen, Jan. I don't want you to worry unnecessarily, but I've called the hospital. Jameson agrees with me that we ought to admit Debbie right away. There's little doubt in my mind that she has pancreatitis.''

"Oh, God, David. No," Janina wailed.

"Take it easy, love. She's going to be all right. It's just a precaution.''

"Oh, damn your doctor talk. It's serious. We both know it. There's no such thing as simple pancreatitis. Let go of me. I want to see her.''

David held her tightly. "Then get hold of yourself. You're going to frighten her without reason. We just have preliminary symptoms, Janina. We want to start treatment immediately so that the disease won't advance.''

His calm tone of voice brought her to her senses. "I'm sorry. You're right. I'm okay now. Let go of me, David, and I'll help her get ready.''

"Good girl.''

Chapter Nine

Less than five minutes later, they were ready to leave for the hospital. Doug looked like a beaten puppy dog. He stayed very close to Debbie, as if by being there he could make her get well.

"Is it okay if I leave my dad's truck here and ride with you?"

"Of course. We hoped you would," Janina said.

Doug held Debbie in his arms in the back of the Mercedes all the way to the hospital. She seemed more relaxed in a forward position. Doug supported her as if she were made of precious porcelain.

Janina was surprised at Debbie's courage. She made Janina promise not to call her parents, at least not until some decision was made about keeping her in the hospital. It occurred to Janina that Debbie was stronger and more considerate than the family gave her credit for. No doubt some of her strength came from Doug. Then, of course, there was David.

Janina marveled that she herself had become so dependent. She had always been the strong one, the person everyone looked to to maintain composure. But now, when one of her own was in trouble.... She squeezed her eyes shut and breathed a silent prayer.

Dr. Jameson was waiting for them in ER when they arrived. He shooed the three of them into a small private waiting room while Debbie underwent the initial examination. It was the longest wait Janina had ever had. Doug was even more anxious, if that was possible. Finally, Dr. Jameson came in.

"Relax, folks. While Debbie does appear to have all the symptoms of pancreatitis, it has not developed to the acute stage."

He shoved his stethoscope into his pocket, then came over and sat down beside Janina. "The feet," he apologized, his shaggy gray eyebrows meeting across the top of his nose. "I've been on them all day. Now, there is no doubt she needs to be hospitalized for a few days. We have to monitor fluids and medications. The one factor that bothers us is her use of alcohol. That has to stop."

Doug nodded. "She's not an alcoholic, but she got in with a wild crowd and they liked to party."

Jameson nodded. "So she said. Well, I think she's learned her lesson on that score. We need to keep close watch over her, but I think we've caught this in time to prevent any permanent damage."

"May we see her now, Dr. Jameson?" Janina asked.

"Of course, for a little while. After that we'll be wanting to get her settled in a room and let her rest. Doctor?" He looked questioningly at David. "I've been wanting to talk to you. If you have a minute?"

David touched Janina's arm. "You and Doug go ahead. I'll meet you at the car."

Janina nodded, more than a trifle uneasy. There was something a little too pat about the way Jameson maneuvered David into a private conversation. Was here something he wasn't telling her? She pasted a confident smile on her face as she walked into ER number 7, where Debbie was waiting.

DAVID WAS WAITING by the Mercedes when Janina got back there. She had taken an extra few minutes to look in on Mr. Fairfax, but he was sleeping. Doug insisted on staying at the hospital in case Debbie needed him, and if she didn't, he planned to visit his father. He said he would pick up his dad's truck the next day.

They had no more than left the parking lot when Janina confronted David. "All right, David. Let's have it."

He tried to be noncommittal, but it didn't work. She saw through him at once. "What did Jameson have to say?"

"Nothing to worry about as far as Debbie is concerned. He was afraid he might cause you undue worry, that's all."

"I'm going to worry a lot more if you don't hurry up and tell me."

"It's not a question of diagnosis. Jameson is about ninety-nine percent sure she has pancreatitis. Of course, he can't be positive until they get the serum amylase tests back." David stuck his lower lip out as if he was considering how to phrase his words. "What Jameson can't figure out is the reason for her attack. He says the damage from alcohol intake is not sufficient in her case to have been an initial cause. Of course, it increased her tendency toward the infection."

Janina's heart gave a lurch. "The malathion substitute."

David shook his head. "No. It seems to be a bacterial infection."

"That's ridiculous. Where would she have gotten it?"

David shrugged. "Almost anywhere. Debbie leads an active life. So far, Jameson hasn't been able to determine whether or not the bacteria is a contributing factor, but he plans to try to isolate and identify it."

Janina slumped against the car door. "Let's get out of here, David. It's too much. I just can't think about it any more."

David looked across at her. Debbie's illness had hit her pretty hard, that on top of everything else. It wasn't like Janina to block things out of her mind. She was the kind who faced things straight on. But now she looked drawn and tired. It pulled a sympathetic chord and he wanted to hold her and take care of her forever.

Janina managed to maintain her self-control until after she showered and slipped into a pale-blue silk robe. She had just loosened the terry-cloth towel from her hair when her foot collided with a fuzzy stuffed toy rabbit that Debbie had brought back from the beach.

She held it up to her cheek and thought about her sister, one minute the sophisticated seventeen-year-old, the next minute, a pink-cheeked, dewy-eyed little girl. No matter what they said, Debbie could die. Janina could hold it in no longer. With a muffled cry of pain, she threw herself on the bed and burst into tears. It was there that David found her.

The bed shifted with his weight as he sat down beside her and laid his hand on her shoulder. "Nina, love," he whispered. "My poor darling. I want to help you."

His hand moved down below her shoulders, easing the tightness in her muscles, making her feel cozy and warm...and cherished. Yes, that was it. David, with a word or a touch, could make her believe that she was the only woman in the world he could ever love. If only it were true. But having him here with her, having him care about her feelings, was more than she would have dared ask for.

Her tears had stopped, and she was left with an emptiness that was as vast as a moonless sky. David stroked her arms, her shoulders, her back, then cupped her breasts in loving gentleness. Healing hands, she thought as she felt the power of them permeate her body to the very center of her being. She sensed that he was holding back, moving slowly to give her time to catch up or change her mind, if need be.

What made him so strong that he could pace himself this way? She knew from the sound of his breathing that he wanted her more than he ever had before. Yet he put her needs before his own. Surely that must be an indication of his love for her.

She ran her hand along his arm, brushing the fine hair with her palm and sending twin currents of passion through their bodies. His face was smooth as if he had just shaved. Her finger traced his jawline. He turned slightly, catching her finger in his mouth and teasing it with his tongue. She was stimulated by the unexpected intimacy. When he released her finger, he captured her hand in his and slowly kissed her palm while his tongue traced small circles in the center.

Then, with seductive patience, his mouth wove an erotic tapestry over her body until she was lifted to uncharted heights of pleasure. She felt her worries slipping away like so many motes of dust in the setting sun, as she became sensitized to the need that had so long lain dormant within her.

Once she had told David that when the time came

for him to make love to her, they would know. The time *had* come, and they both knew it.

Janina didn't have to wonder if David was ready. His eyes blazed with an intensity fueled by a passion that had been banked for three years. But now that passion could not long be held in check. He had called her Nina, as he often had in moments of love. Now, the mere sound of it sent tongues of flame coursing through her, and she rolled onto her back, reaching out to him and pulling him down beside her.

It came as only a small surprise that he wore only his pajama bottom, but the knowledge served to inflame her already-heated blood. He brushed aside her robe and lightly kissed her shoulder, then drifted moist kisses across the hollow at the base of her throat and along the ridge of her collarbone.

Her robe had come undone, and as he leaned over her, the hair on his chest, springy-damp from the shower, brushed against the soft curve of her bosom. Her breasts peaked with an aching desire, hardening against his chest until he moaned with hunger.

Janina's arms wound around his neck as his mouth found hers in a searing kiss that engulfed their simmering passions. She gave him pleasure for pleasure as his hands rediscovered the tiny, intimate recesses of her body. Her own hands tore at the snaps to his pajama bottom and he managed to shuck free of them without interrupting their kiss. Her robe had long since been thrown to the foot of the bed in a careless heap.

Time had not embroidered Janina's memories. David had been the one to awaken her core of sensuality and he was the one man who could evoke, once again, that fundamental, primitive urgency. She wanted him with a longing that turned to liquid inside of her, a need that pushed reason aside in its drive for satisfaction.

"Nina, Nina," he whispered against the lower curve of her chin. "Don't you see how right it is for us to be together?" She lifted her head, and his lips caressed her throat. When she could stand it no longer, she lowered her mouth to his and kissed him deeply. His mouth was warm and soft with loving, his breath gentle against her cheek. It was as if he had never been away. She wound her arms around him, pulling him still closer until their bodies curved into each other to form a bonding that was as natural as life itself.

She felt radiant with power she had over him, a power that she returned to him in full measure. The radiance surged through her veins, igniting her blood to fever pitch, until it was unbearable.

"David," she whispered his name aloud. He smiled, knowing that she had come home to him again, and his eyes reflected his absolute joy.

He moved over her then, firmly but gently, and they came together like the joining of equal parts that lose only in separation. Their need was too intense for them to delay long the culmination of their passion. They rose together like eagles soaring aloft on a single current of air, then floated downward in lazy, sensual delight.

Janina drifted back little by little. The emptiness was gone. She was filled with a sense of euphoria as she continued to hold David in her arms. David relaxed slowly, his breathing gradually becoming less strained. He bent his head and kissed her softly on the mouth, in gratitude and wonderment that two people could be so unbelievably attuned to each other.

She curled her hand at the back of his neck, stroking

the tiny hollow by his shoulders. They lay there for a while in each other's arms. It felt right to Janina. It was where she belonged. And yet some inner voice accused her of using David to get her through this period of emotional trauma. She reached over to stroke his cheek with her knuckles.

"Thank you for waiting, David. I know it wasn't easy. I . . . I don't know how to explain what I'm feeling right now." She rested her head on his bare chest, and he could feel her breath ripple across the tightly curled mat of hair.

She took a deep breath and slowly expelled it. "I somehow feel that I used you, took advantage of your being here when I needed you. I didn't mean it that way. You surely must know how much I care for you."

He leaned up on one elbow and supported his head on his hand. "Listen, love. Haven't you figured out yet that I want to be there when you need me? That doesn't mean just the good times. Just the times in our lives when we're young and slim and full of energy and sex." He ruffled her hair. "Although that isn't half-bad." He leaned down and brushed his mouth across her lips. "I want to be with you when your hair turns gray and the wrinkles line your cheeks and sex happens only on our ninety-fifth-plus anniversaries."

Janina smiled. "Will you still cook for me?"

"I sure won't let you cook for me. I plan to live to a ripe old age."

She grabbed his face in her hands and held on to it firmly. "Then I'd advise you to quit making cracks about my cooking. After all, I do have other talents."

"That you do, lady, that you do," he said as he rolled over and pulled her toward him. "Oh, Janina, I adore the way you feel against my skin."

They lay there contentedly for a while, talking about things they used to do when they were together. And then they made love again. This time the urgency was diluted somewhat and they were able to take their time and make all the stops along the way toward that incredible summit. Afterward, they showered together and returned to Janina's bed.

David rolled over to face her, his hand caressing the smoothness of her thigh. "Janina. There's something I want to ask you. I've put it off this long because I was afraid you'd refuse me, but I can't go on without knowing. I want to marry you, Janina. Will you—"

She put her fingers over his lips. "Wait, David," she protested. "Don't ask me now."

He looked stunned. "Why not?"

"Well, what are we going to tell our children when they ask where we were when you proposed?"

He slowly let his breath out, then chuckled softly. "We can always say that we were doing calisthenics."

"Be serious. I mean it, David. I've waited a long time for this. I want a proper proposal in a proper setting."

She couldn't tell him that she also wanted to know beyond a doubt that it wasn't something that occurred to him just because they happened to make love. He seemed to sense it, because he didn't argue, or even laugh at her as he might have done.

"All right, love, if that's what you want. But first you have to promise that you'll say yes."

"You can count on it."

"Then get up and get dressed."

"Now?"

"Wear something pretty and ladylike that won't embarrass our children when we talk about it years from now."

"David!"

He grinned and got up off the bed. "I'll give you thirty minutes."

SHE WAS READY in twenty-five. David watched her come into the den, fresh, vibrant and beautifully alive. His voice was husky when he reached for her hand. "I'm beginning to think maybe you aren't so crazy after all, love. You look exquisite."

She felt surrounded by a warm glow. It had been worth dragging the pale-pink linen dress out of its garment bag, putting on pantyhose, jewelry and a touch of mascara. For a while she was afraid she had overdone it, but seeing him in his three-piece gray suit, pale-blue shirt and matching striped tie, she knew it was perfect.

"Ready?" he asked as he took her hand and led her out the door toward his Mercedes.

"Where are we going this time of night?"

"You'll see. Just behave yourself."

"The expressway?" she asked as they entered the approach to Foothill Boulevard. She was getting concerned. David could be such a character sometimes. For all she knew, he might plan to be gone a week.

She looked up at him. "At the risk of spoiling everything, I can't go far, David. There's Debbie...and I'm trying to decide about calling my parents, but I think it's too late."

"Trust me." He grinned. It was obvious that he was enjoying himself.

They continued to drive for another short distance until they came to Stevens Creek Boulevard, then turned right on Saratoga/Sunnyvale Road and proceeded on toward Big Basin Way.

David slowed the car to compensate for the narrow, curved road, then made a sharp turn at the top of a hill and pulled into a deserted grove of gnarled trees. Janina caught her breath. The view overlooked the cities at night: Sunnyvale, Santa Clara, Willowbrook and part of San Jose. The flickering lights, haloed by the evening dampness, were like millions of dewdrops spread out on a carpet of cobalt blue.

David got out of the car and came around to open her door. Janina was struck by the profound silence, but more impressive was the scent of magnolias mixed with evergreens and orange blossoms.

"I remember this place!" she said, clasping her hands together. "We came here the night I took you to meet my parents."

The moon was bright enough that she could see the happiness flooding his face in an ear-to-ear grin. "Yeah. I was afraid you'd forgotten."

"No. I'd never forget that. I remember we stayed here so long that the early morning fog came rolling in over the mountain and it was like being wrapped in our own private cocoon."

David put his arm around her and guided her up an old stone pathway, which was cushioned with pale-green lichen. They stopped at the ruins of a small cottage that stood at the brink of a steep hillside overlooking the ravine. "I should have brought a blanket so we could sit on the steps."

"I'll take a chance if you will." She brushed the sprinkling of pine needles away and sat down, leaving room for him beside her.

His knee brushed hers as he reached for her hand. When he spoke, his voice was husky with emotion. "Janina, for the sake of our children, and our children's children, and all of those who follow after us, I want to make this a moment to remember.''

She wasn't sure whether to laugh or cry, but tears gathered behind her eyelids as he dug into his pocket and brought out a square velvet box. He opened it, revealing a simple but elegant, square-cut diamond ring. "I love you, Jan. I've always loved you. Even when it looked like we didn't have a chance. But now we have." He brought her hand to his lips and when he spoke again his voice trembled. "Janina Scott, will you do me the honor of becoming my wife?"

"Oh, David," she murmured as he slipped the ring onto her finger. It was all she could do to speak. "The answer is yes, yes! I love you, too, and always have . . . and always will."

He cupped her face in his hands and kissed her sweetly on the mouth. Janina didn't want him to know that she had tears in her eyes, but he reached over and brushed them away with his thumbs. It was all right, though, because when he kissed her again, she saw that his eyes, too, were filled with tears.

He held her in his arms for a long time as they watched the city lights disappear like fireflies in the night. It grew cool, and he draped his jacket around her shoulders, but she moved closer so that it served them both.

"Comfortable?" he asked.

"Um. Perfect. I'd like to stay here forever."

"Dawn will be here in a little while."

"I know, but I hate to have the night end. This was a beautiful thing you did, David." She smiled radiantly. "I have a feeling our children and grandchildren will be proud of us."

He grinned. "I hope so. At any rate, I look forward to finding out."

They stayed for perhaps another hour, talking quietly, kissing, touching. Janina savored each minute as further proof that this was really happening and not simply a passing dream born of her need for David. Finally, they walked back to the car and headed toward the condominium.

Neither of them was able to sleep after they returned home. They sat together on David's bed in the den and listened to the stereo and tried to make plans. David lay with his head in Janina's lap. With her finger, she traced the fine contour of his shaggy brows, coaxing the stragglers into place, smoothing the worry line at the center of his forehead.

She wondered aloud. "What will your father say about our getting married, David?"

"I know he'll be pleased. I've written him about you many times. He was upset...because of Susan, and I don't think he ever understood. Partly, I guess, because he was preconditioned to be on your side because he knew I loved you. I want him to get to know you, but I doubt if he can fly home from London for the wedding. But as soon as we set a date, I plan to cable him."

"Is he like you?"

"No. More sensible and a little stuffy, I guess. The typical accountant type."

"I like him already."

"Will your parents be happy about the fact that we are getting together at last?"

She laughed. "The getting together could have been a problem. Our *marriage*, on the other hand, is what they've always wanted for me. Of course they'll be happy."

He prodded her gently. "Even if I'm disgustingly wealthy?"

She was faintly embarrassed, remembering a previous conversation. "Face it, David. Nothing's perfect. We'll have to learn to live with it."

"We've a lot of decisions to make. Can you bear leaving Northern California for San Diego? It means disposing of your house, giving up your job."

She laughed sharply. "What job? At the moment, I'm in limbo. Not much to want to hold on to."

"If you want to work, I'm sure you can find a job at Cedar Valley Hospital, with me. Or when my clinic opens, you could work there. You said you were particularly interested in preventative medicine."

She nuzzled his ear with her nose. "I wouldn't mind taking a year or two off to stay home and make a baby."

"Good idea. Maybe we should start practicing." He pulled her down next to him and began kissing her with undisguised fervor.

In the relentless sunlight of the following day, the splendor of the night before seemed like fragments from a transient dream. It became reality when Janina touched the shimmering diamond ring on her left hand, but even then she had difficulty convincing herself it was really true.

Marriage to David! It was what she had wanted from that first day on the beach at Carmel. She had been so happy then, but happiness was as fragile as a whiff of spindrift on the sand. It had escaped her. Now she held it close against her breast, savoring the warm sensations that lifted her soul and made her feel incredibly, wondrously alive with anticipation.

True, there were a few chips in her cup of happiness, but time would take care of that. First there was Debbie to worry about, and then the reason behind Debbie's being in the hospital. Now that Debbie was involved, it became even more crucial to get to the bottom of it.

Janina suddenly remembered the remark Dr. Jameson had made to David about finding traces of bacteria. She had been too upset at the time to think much about it, but now she wanted to know if Dr. Jameson had learned anything else. It probably wasn't significant, since none of the other doctors had reported unusual bacterial infections.

While David was in the shower, she called the hospital to talk to Dr. Jameson, but he was making rounds and was not available. The floor nurse said that Debbie had spent a restless night but she was not experiencing pain. A good sign, Janina thought, but she was eager to talk to the doctor. She called Debbie's room and spoke briefly, just barely avoiding spilling the news about her engagement to David. It seemed only right that her parents be the first to know.

Doug was with Debbie. No doubt the two of them were driving the nurses crazy. Doug was beginning to relax a little now that Mr. Fairfax's condition continued to improve.

After Janina talked to Debbie, she decided to call her parents and tell them about Debbie's condition...and her own good fortune. They took both the good and the bad news with typical stoicism and made arrangements to go to the hospital before noon to see Debbie.

David was a little apprehensive about seeing Janina's parents, but Janina convinced him there was nothing to worry about. They met her parents at the hospital and took them to lunch. Now that the engagement was official, her father warmed up quickly and proceeded to give the two of them his blessing along with an abundance of advice. Later the Scotts accompanied Doug up to see his father on another floor. They liked Doug and, better yet, liked the fact that he was seeing Debbie again. Doug had been a little concerned that they would hold him responsible for Debbie's illness.

Debbie was delighted by the news of Janina's engagement to David and wanted to know when they planned to get married. Janina was at a loss to know what to say.

It was hard to equate her present euphoria with the things that were going on in her life. It was as if she existed on two levels, the real and the superreal. Coming down to the decisions of real life wasn't going to be easy. David wanted to get married as soon as possible, but Janina felt that loose ends had to be tied up first. She couldn't divide herself up into pieces, worrying over Debbie's condition on one hand, while at the same time planning a wedding, even though she hoped to keep it simple. Then there was also the concern over the pancreatitis incidents, not to mention decisions to be made about her job.

IT WAS A CHANCE REMARK by Doug that caught Janina's and David's interest. While she and David were standing in the corridor talking to him, Doug casually mentioned that one of the residents at the nursing home where he worked part-time had just been admitted with pancreatitis. When they questioned him more closely, they learned that the woman was in her seventies, was nonambulatory and, except for a broken hip, was in otherwise good health. She had not been out of the nursing home in over two months

"But, David, that can't be," Janina said. "If that's true, then the malathion substitute couldn't be—" She drew a sharp breath. "Wait a minute. I just thought of something. Remember the men at the staging site?"

He nodded. "Vaguely. There was nothing special about them that I recall."

"Don't you see? That's just the point. Why did the men at Langtree Labs wear protective clothing if Levi's were adequate protection for the men on the tank trucks?"

David swore softly. "That's it. I knew there was something that seemed out of focus, but I couldn't put my finger on it."

Doug looked bewildered. "You guys lost me. What staging site? What protective clothing?"

David looked apologetic. "Let's go into that another time. For now, I think we can scratch the idea that the new insecticide is responsible for the infections."

"But what, then?" Janina asked. "What on earth is it that all these cases have in common? Just what is the red string that ties the nursing home in with the other cases?"

"It isn't likely to be their diet," Doug said, scratching his head. "The nursing home conforms to strict regulations. They prepare all the food in the kitchen. Besides, only Mrs. Kalmer, out of dozens of other patients, became sick."

He shook his head. "She is such a sweet old lady. I always spend a lot of time with her when I'm finished with my work." His forehead creased in frustration. "Why is it that the people I care for most in the world have to be sick?"

David's eyes opened wide and his jaw dropped.

"But that's it! My God, why didn't we see it before? Doug is the connection."

"Hey, wait a minute, David. Are you trying to tell me I'm going around infecting people with pancreatitis?"

David could have kicked himself for being so blunt. Doug looked devastated as David reached out to touch his shoulder. "Doug, I didn't mean it to sound..."

He shook his head in disbelief. "No, there's no way you can convince me I'm some kind of Typhoid Mary. I don't see how it could be true. I don't have pancreatitis. I've never had it."

Janina pressed her hands together. "Wait a minute. David might have something. The cases originally centered around Langtree Labs, where the county has been spraying heavily for the fruit fly."

David interrupted. "Look, why don't we go outside? We're attracting an awful lot of attention." Patients and visitors as well as staff members walking by were casting curious looks as the conversation became animated. Janina nodded and David piloted them toward a narrow deck that ran along the exterior of one side of the building.

They were barely outside the door when David spoke again. "When your dad got sick, we began to discount our theory that Langtree was involved, but then you told us that he had been working at Langtree recently and that altered the picture."

Doug nodded, still looking confused and a little defensive.

Janina walked over to the concrete railing and rested her elbows on it. "Naturally, we assumed that your father had been exposed to the new kind of spray they are using. But then Debbie and the patient from the convalescent home became ill, and we had to reassess our theory again.''

David softly smacked his fist against his palm in obvious agitation. "Okay. The lab is the connection to the disease, you're the connection to the lab. I'd stake my life on it. But how? Have you ever worked at Langtree?''

"Never. I went to see a man at Langtree about Dad's work, but I was only there for a few minutes.'' His face was a mixture of outrage, frustration and confusion. "There has to be something else that's responsible. I couldn't have—''

"Oh," Janina groaned. "The truck! Debbie said you drive your dad's truck when you take her on a date.''

Doug nodded, looking sheepish. "Well, yeah. I can't afford a car right now, but I don't see how—''

"Debbie told me once that the truck is full of air-conditioning equipment. You said your dad had replaced some filters in the New Products Lab. Do you know what he did with the filters he removed?''

"Put them in the truck, I suppose. They must still be there." His eyes widened as comprehension set in.

David whistled. "You've got it, Janina." He looked around as if to make certain no one could hear. "Now I remember Jameson saying something about the presence of some unidentified submicroscopic bacteria. It's not the spray that's the problem. We've been approaching from the wrong angle." He lowered his voice. "*It's what they're spraying for!* I'll bet they've isolated a new form of bacteria and some of it got away from them. The spray is not an insecticide, as we assumed, but some kind of bactericide.''

Janina nodded, afraid to speak. David was right. She was convinced of it. Doug stared at them in disbelief.

"I hope you guys know what you're saying. My God, if word of this got out—whether or not it's true—do you realize what kind of panic we'd have in the town. . .the county?"

Janina protested. "But Doug, we can't just sit back and watch people get sick. We tried to do something about it earlier, but nobody would listen. Langtree owns the town, and the word is apparently out that they want to keep this thing quiet."

"Yeah, I know how that goes. I used to work with an environmental group until I ran out of steam. We went to press, to the radio and TV." He snapped his fingers. "Zilch. The only encouragement we got was from the community-access programming staff of cable TV, and they never really did anything outstanding. Just a token gesture."

David turned his back to the railing and leaned against it. "I was about convinced we ought to give up the struggle, but now I don't see how we can."

"We can't!" Janina affirmed. "Not when we consider all the consequences. But what can we do that we haven't already done?"

David broke the long silence. "For one thing, Doug. You'd better stop driving your dad's truck until we find out more about this whole thing."

Janina offered the use of her car, and though Doug was reluctant, she rummaged in her purse and handed him the keys. "Better make sure the truck is locked up tight when you get back to my place."

Doug shoved his hands in his pockets. "I still can't figure this thing out. If everyone else is getting sick, why aren't we? And how about the other patients in the nursing home?''

"Good question," David mused. "I wish I had an answer. I'd like to know what is different about your friend's case, how it differs from the other patients at the convalescent home."

They continued to discuss the subject and what to do about it until Doug went back into the hospital to be with Debbie. Even afterward, David and Janina explored their options and came up dry.

"Maybe if we sleep on it, we'll think of something," David said.

Later, as Janina and David, in cutoff jeans, were lounging on her patio, she traced a path along his thigh with her fingertip and wondered that life could change so drastically from moment to moment.

"David, what made you decide at that particular moment to take a leave of absence? I mean, Susan had been dead for a few months. You might have come earlier, or you might have waited longer." She nudged him playfully. "I'm not complaining. Just wondering what triggered the decision."

He leaned over and kissed the place just below her ear. "I kept thinking about you, wondering if you remembered me...and could understand why I did what I did. For a while I was afraid to know the answer, but as time went on I knew I couldn't wait another day."

He ran his hand down the slim length of her. "And I kept thinking about the way your curves fit against my hollow places, and how your hair smells of lemon after you wash it." His fingers found the tiny buttons on the front of her blouse and undid them, punctuating each movement downward with teasings by mouth and tongue. He gloried in the clean cool taste of her and the way her body arched toward him in response.

"Janina, I'd like to set a date for our wedding. Soon. Before I have to go back to San Diego. That way we can go back there together."

"But that's about two weeks."

"I know it's a long time to wait—"

"A long time! David, tell me you're joking. I can't be ready in two weeks."

"Sure you can. I'll help. But I need to call my father so he can try to arrange a flight from London. How about the twenty-third?"

Her voice was tremulous. "All right. Good heavens. I can't believe I'm saying this." She studied his face and saw the love and happiness shining from his eyes. If he had suggested it, she would have married him that night.

"Could we be married in my parents' church, do you suppose?"

David cupped her face in his hands. "I'd like that." He pulled a lock of her hair. "Besides, it's better than being married on a raft going over Niagara Falls, or something like that. Our children will appreciate our respectability."

"Don't be a smarty. We have to think ahead, you know."

"I am. I'm thinking about your condo. Would you like to give it to Debbie and Doug if they decide to get married?"

"Oh, David. Could we really afford that? I'd love to." Then she began to think more clearly. "But maybe it would be smarter not to make it too easy for them. Maybe we could let them buy it for a low price over a long period of time."

"Fine with me. And your job? When will you give your notice?"

Janina smiled grimly. "I'll hand in my resignation tomorrow or the day after. It should make my replacement happy, not to mention Randolph Baker. Damn! It makes me mad that he could get away with aiding the cover-up. A hospital, of all things."

They were silent for several minutes and David sensed her withdrawal.

"What's troubling you, love?" he asked, kissing her forehead.

"I can't stop thinking about the cover-up. Let's go in to see the mayor tomorrow. If he knows that we know everything, maybe he'll agree to take a stand. Somehow we've got to stop Langtree from carrying out dangerous experiments in a populated neighborhood without using proper precautions."

"I'll go with you to see the mayor, Janina, but I doubt that it's going to do any good. He'll probably refuse to see us."

"He'll see us."

BUT JANINA WAS LESS SURE OF HERSELF after reaching the mayor's office by phone the following morning.

"I'm sorry, Ms Scott," his secretary said. "Mayor Allen is in, but his appointment book is jammed and he is unable to come to the telephone at the moment."

"Just tell him that I want to discuss bacteria," Janina said.

An instant later the mayor picked up the phone. "This is Mayor Allen. If I remember correctly, you are patient coordinator at Mercy General, Ms Scott. Now, what is it that is so important you have to interrupt a conference?"

"I don't think we ought to talk over the phone, Mr. Mayor. I'd like to see you at your office this morning."

"For what reason?"

"I have proof of the cover-up."

He laughed, but there was no sound of humor in his voice. "I heard that you were creating something of a disturbance and had been suspended from the hospital staff. If you will forgive me, there is nothing I can do to help you."

"We have the filters, Mr. Mayor."

There was an excruciating silence. Finally he spoke. "Let me warn you, young lady. If you make a statement like that and don't have anything to back it up, it will take you the rest of your life to pay off our lawsuit, assuming you don't spend the rest of your life in jail."

"I told you we—I have the filters. Don't worry. They're safe. No one has touched them since Mr. Fairfax removed them."

"I hope you realize, Ms Scott, that you are putting yourself in a very precarious position by your threatening remarks."

"When can we talk, Mr. Mayor?"

"I'll get back to you this afternoon. Uh...where can I reach you?"

She gave him her telephone number. "I'll wait until two o'clock to hear from you," she said. But the line had already gone dead. It was just as well. Her hands were shaking so hard that she couldn't have held on for another minute.

"Oh, Lord. I did it. How did it sound? Do you think I did the right thing?"

David shrugged. "You did all right. I just hope you won't be sorry." He looked worried.

Janina's breath caught in her throat. "What do you mean?"

"I don't know. It's just a thought, but I have a feeling he's stalling." He put his arm around Janina's waist and she linked her fingers with his.

"We have the proof, David. They can't stop us now, can they?" He didn't answer and somehow his silence was more ominous than a flat denial might have been.

Chapter Ten

Janina looked apprehensive. "What do you mean, you think the mayor might be stalling? Do you think he might try to have me arrested?"

"I doubt it," David said. "Too much chance of having the story go public. I just have a gut feeling that he wants time to jockey for position."

"But what can he do, David? We have the truck with the filters. That's all the proof we need. They're powerless to do anything."

"I hope you're right. Anyway, we'll know more when he calls back."

"I don't think I can stand it until then. The time is really going to drag."

He went down on one knee and buried his head in her lap. "Stick with me, love. We'll find some way to make it fly."

They spent the rest of the morning trying to avoid looking at the telephone. David was wrong, though. The clock moved slowly despite the fact that they kept each other entertained.

Janina couldn't have managed without David. He was an angel about helping around the house, but she decided she had better draw the line when he volunteered to water her plants. Either that or her African violets would have to start wearing hip boots. The poor things were floating in an inch of water he'd drawn from the tap, yet! When she pointed out her special jug of pure, unsoftened water from the patio faucet, he stepped back in mock horror.

"Good heavens! Do we perform a transfusion here or take them to the emergency room?"

"Idiot. They'll survive this time, but if we continued to use house water, the salt from the water softener would kill them."

"How did you learn so much about plants?"

"Experience. I love working in the garden more than I like working in the house. But then you already knew that. How can you marry a woman who can't cook?" she asked sadly.

He pulled her into his arms until she was pressed firmly against him from her knees to her neck. "I'd rather have a wife who makes things grow."

She leaned back in surprise. "I didn't know you were that crazy about plants."

"Who said anything about plants?" He grinned as he cupped her hips in his hands and held her close. The intimate contact with his body left no doubt as to what he meant.

"David Madison, you are impossible." She laughed as she unbuttoned his shirt and slowly ran her tongue across the tangle of dark hair on his chest. "Impossible but right. I'm the first one to admit that I have a passion for growing things."

He kissed the top of her head. "I'd carry you off to bed, but I have the feeling you would be distracted. Want me to fix lunch?"

She marveled at his sensitivity. Much as she loved

David, she couldn't stop thinking about the mayor's impending phone call. While David was working his magic at the stove, Janina turned the television to the local cable TV program. They were showing a meeting of the Department of Parks and Recreation, which was campaigning for more parks in the town.

Janina watched with interest. "Fascinating. Do you have the feeling they're each trying to see who gets the most air time?"

"It's good publicity as long as they are all in agreement."

"I'll bet if something controversial came up, they'd all find a way of hiding their faces from the camera."

David looked thoughtful. "Well, if they're doing it the way they used to when I was a witness in the hearings on sports injuries in the schools, they might not even know which person the camera is filming. The camera and audio crews work from a projection room to avoid disrupting the proceedings."

"That's surprising. I would have guessed the cameras were right there in front of the people."

"Well, if Teddy Liederbach is still running the camera, I can see why. He used to be a cameraman for ABC in New York but he wanted to move back to the Bay Area, so he gave up the extra money to be able to live in California."

"His name sounds familiar. I think I've seen it on the list of credits." She rinsed the carrots she had been scraping and put them in a bowl of ice cubes. "They keep talking about the article in today's paper about the parks initiative. Come to think of it, I forgot to bring the paper in."

David grinned. "I'm surprised old Gary didn't train the cat to do it."

Janina gave him a scathing look as she went outside

to pick up the paper. A moment later she dashed back into the house.

"David. It's gone!"

He was surprised by the intensity of her expression. "What's gone? The paper?"

"My God, no. I mean the truck. It's not there. I know Doug wouldn't have taken it. It must have been stolen."

David dried his hands on a towel. "Well, now we know why the mayor was stalling. There goes our evidence."

Janina's stomach felt as if someone had kicked her. Just when she thought they were beginning to make progress, they were pushed backward. "But what can we do? And what about Doug's truck?"

He blew a stream of air out of his mouth. "I suppose we'd better have Doug report the vehicle as stolen, but my guess is that whoever took it has it stashed out of sight. Probably somewhere at one of the Langtree facilities."

Janina was sick with disappointment. "The mayor was just playing games with me, wasn't he? He isn't going to call, is he, David?"

"I doubt it very much." He put his arms around her. "I guess it's true that you can't fight city hall...in this town, anyway."

Janina melted against him. "Damn. I'm so tired of this whole mess. All I want to do is get married and go away with you and forget about everything else for a while."

"It's fine with me, love, but I don't think you can forget it that easily. I know you. You don't like to leave anything unfinished."

"Nor do you," she said, looking up at him.

He kissed the top of her nose. "I guess we're two of a kind."

She lifted her lips to his and they kissed deeply, holding each other as if they were afraid to let go.

After a while Janina called the hospital and reached Doug just as he arrived. He agreed to report the theft of the truck, and Janina was grateful that he refrained from asking too many questions over the phone. After she hung up, she called the mayor's office and was told that he had left the office for the day. When Janina asked if he had left a message for her, the secretary hesitated.

"No, I'm afraid not."

"Did he say anything about planning to call me?"

"No, Ms. Scott. He didn't mention it."

"All right. I'll call him first thing tomorrow morning."

"Oh, he won't be available. The mayor has a ribbon-cutting ceremony at the new library annex. It will tie him up all morning."

"Then how about the afternoon?"

"I'm sorry. He has a meeting on schedule and I don't know how long it will last."

"It couldn't last more than two hours, could it? It's vital that I speak to him in person."

"I wish I could help you, Ms Scott, but the meeting is a special one in the council chambers. I wouldn't normally tell you that, but since it seems so urgent that you see him..."

Janina hesitated. "No, that's all right. I understand. I—I'm on staff at the hospital."

"I see. That explains."

"Yes. I suspect you're talking about his meeting with the Langtree people and the members of the board that's set for one P.M."

"That's right. I—wait a minute. Wasn't it for one-thirty?"

Janina pretended to shuffle some papers. "Good heavens, you're right. One-thirty it is. It's getting so I can't read my own writing." She forced a laugh. "All right. Thank you. My business will have to wait, I suppose. Thank you again."

Janina hung up the receiver and shook her head. "Well, that does it. The mayor has left for the day. He must know that without the filters we don't have any substantial proof." She hated to face David. "I should never have told him about the filters. It was stupid. How could I have been so naïve?"

"Don't blame yourself. You did the best anyone could."

"But it wasn't good enough. Damn! I'm beginning to think I can't do anything right."

He put his arm across her shoulders. "Cut it out. You expect yourself to be perfect. Nobody's perfect, Janina."

"I did find out one thing, though. The mayor is having an important meeting with the Langtree group and some of the members of the city council tomorrow afternoon at one-thirty."

"I'd sure like to be a mouse in a corner and hear what they say. It has to be a strategy meeting about the latest developments in the case."

"I'm sure of it. Wait . . . I have an idea." She grabbed the phone and dialed the direct number of the hospital administrator's secretary. When the woman answered, Janina made a heroic attempt to disguise her voice.

"This is Mayor Allen's office. I'm just calling to remind Mr. Baker about his meeting here at city hall for tomorrow at one-thirty."

There was a pause. "Yes. He has it written in on the appointment calendar. Thank you for calling."

Janina slowly replaced the receiver, then dialed the office of the editor of the *Sentinel* with the same results.

"I knew it. Damn! Everyone who is anyone in town is going to be there. I think we should go, too."

David grinned. "Lady, you don't kid around. Do you have any idea what you're getting us into?"

She walked over and put her arms around him. "Oh, David. I love you so much. I'd give anything to go, but I know they'd never let us in."

They were standing there holding each other when the doorbell rang. It was Doug.

"I did what you guys suggested and called the police to report the stolen truck," he said. There was a breathless kind of excitement in his voice as he paused. "Then about five minutes before I left the hospital, some guy came in to question me about the filters. I told him I didn't know anything."

"Was he from the police department?" David asked.

"He didn't say when I asked him. Anyway, he didn't learn anything he didn't know." He paused again. "But I think I've found the answer. I think I figured out why some of the people seem to be prone to the infection. I could be wrong, but I think I'm right. I've weighed all the reasons for and against, and I can't see any flaw in my reasoning."

Janina wanted to shake him. "For gosh sakes, what is it, Doug?"

"It's so simple you'll never believe it."

"Doug!" David warned.

"Okay, okay." He sank down into a chair next to

the kitchen table. David and Janina sat down opposite him. His fingers began tapping the table as his gaze jumped from David to Janina.

"I was wrong about my dad never taking a drink. He just told me that he had downed a few beers at a bachelor party they gave for George Hurlburt, the guy who just got married."

Janina started to protest, but Doug brushed it aside as he continued. "And old Mrs. Kalmer, from the convalescent home. She swore she never touched liquor, but I found out she kept a bottle in her dresser drawer for medicinal purposes. When I checked, the bottle was empty and so were two others I found in her nightstand." Doug slapped his fist on the table. "It's got to be the answer. I can feel it in my gut."

Janina shook her head. "I wish it were that simple, but I think you're overlooking some of the cases. Why, for example, did none of the other patients at the convalescent home come down with the disease? I know that the kitchen often serves wine with the meals for some of the private patients. So, if liquor is the connection, why didn't some of the other patients show any symptoms? It just doesn't fit."

Doug slowly wilted as they tore his case apart. "Damn, I was so sure. Then I guess it gets back to me being a carrier. I just can't—"

David leaned his elbows on the table and stared at Doug. "Think about it. What can you tell me about Mrs. Kalmer that's different from all the other patients at the home?"

"Well, I've gotten closer to her than most of the other patients at the convalescent home. Funny, too, because she hasn't been a patient there very long. She was brought in sometime in March, I think. Yeah, that was it. I know because it was just after we had that big hepatitis scare the first part of the year." He ran his fingernail along the crack that separated the table halves. "There isn't anything different about her. She gets the same treatment as anyone else with her symptoms."

"Hepatitis?" David mused, a puzzled expression in his eyes. "Where did I hear that mentioned recently?"

Janina shrugged. "Could have been anywhere. It was running wild for a couple of weeks back in February. They're still talking about it at the hospital. The whole staff was inoculated with gamma globulin."

Doug nodded. "Yeah. We were, too. I guess it got started when they had the rodeo out at the fairgrounds last February."

Janina stiffened. "The fairgrounds! Wait, David. I know where you heard it. Remember the man we met while we were horseback riding? His wife has pancreatitis. He mentioned that he had to have shots against hepatitis because he had been exposed to it when he was working at the fairgrounds."

"That's it." David looked jubilant. "I think we've got it. I've been inoculated, too, as I suppose most people in health-care service have been. If it really is the gamma globulin that protected us from contamination, it's beginning to make sense."

"But what now?" Janina asked. "My God, if they don't take proper precautions with Doug's truck, they could contaminate a lot of people. I wonder if direct contact with the bacteria is necessary." She turned to Doug. "Did Debbie actually touch the filter?"

He nodded. "We both did. It's kinda bulky. We moved it a couple times to make more room in the truck."

David frowned. "That means that anyone who opened the truck while they were moving it might possibly have also picked up the filters."

Doug shook his head. "Not much chance. They towed the truck in. I asked around the complex, and the gardener saw the municipal towing service haul it away. They never even opened the doors." He shoved his hands into the pockets of his jeans. "I called the towing service to find out where the truck is being kept, but they claim they never heard of it. So. . ." He spread his hands. "That's the way it stands as of right now."

"So the police were in on it, too," Janina observed. "Why am I surprised?"

No one answered. Both David and Doug were lost in thought.

"Well, there's at least one consolation," Janina said. "Since they knew that the truck was contaminated, it's not likely that anyone will run the risk of opening it up without taking proper precautions."

They discussed the ways of getting the truck back, but failed to come to any conclusion. Then Doug said he had to go out to his dad's place and pick up some things they had forgotten to pack.

After Doug left, David walked around the house as if he were trying to come to terms with something. It made Janina uneasy. It wasn't like David to be secretive, but something clearly was bothering him.

"Did you send the cablegram to your father?" she asked.

"Uh-huh."

"Did you hear from him?"

"Huh-uh." He didn't bother to look up as he paced across the kitchen and back. Cinnamon rubbed against his leg, but David didn't appear to notice. That was an even greater cause for Janina's concern.

"All right, David. What's wrong?"

He looked up at her as if he had just seen her for the first time. "I—I have a couple of things I want to do before dinner. Come to think about it, I don't think I'll be home for dinner."

"Oh?" Her voice sounded cool and remote, but he didn't appear to notice. It was exasperating. "David, what are you up to?"

He looked vaguely uncomfortable. "It's just an idea I have. Chances are, it won't even work. It's probably a waste of time and energy."

"David Madison! You're beginning to sound like Doug, the way he takes ten minutes to build up to something before he's ready to say it. For heaven's sake, what is it you're planning to do?"

"Look up an old friend of mine."

"Oh."

He grinned as he came over to where she was standing. "Do I detect the presence of the green-eyed monster?"

"I am *not* jealous, David. But I am curious. Can't I go with you?"

"Not this time, love. I'm going to look up a fellow I used to work with. I don't think he'd be too thrilled to have a third person present."

"Now I'm scared instead of simply curious. David, don't do anything foolish."

He put his hands on her shoulders and she leaned into him, loving the warmth of his arms as they enfolded her. She pulled his shirt out of the waistband at the back of his trousers and ran her fingers across his back.

"Don't go, David, please. Stay here with me and we can go to bed and pretend we're married."

He grinned and stepped backward, out of her reach. "Something tells me I'd better leave while I still have the chance." He tucked his shirttail back into his trousers. "Look, Jan, it's nothing. I just have a hunch this guy can help us put an end to this business about the cover-up, but I'd better see him alone."

"All right, David, but be careful and come back as soon as you can."

"I plan to take you up on your offer the minute I get home, and that's a promise."

He kissed her with considerable passion, but there was something missing and Janina guessed that his mind was already on the mysterious man he planned to see.

The minute his car left the parking lot, Janina began to feel apprehensive. Before David had come back, it had never bothered her to be alone. Now the house seemed to be aware of her unease and it creaked and cracked every time she took a step across the floor. In frustration, she turned on the television in time to catch a local news brief. The announcer sounded jubilant.

"And for all you who have backyard orchards, the news from the County Agriculture Department is encouraging. Harvey Rudolph, who has led the fight against the fruit-fly invasion, now believes that the fruit-fly threat has been brought under control and there will be no need to pick those apricots after all. Although aerial spraying will continue for a few more days, it will be on a smaller scale and in only a few selected areas. Once again, credit goes to the men who have worked night and day to bring this fruit-fly invasion under control."

Janina was outraged. "Fruit fly, my foot! If the people only knew how they had been fooled by the cover-up." *Anyway,* she thought, *they must be pretty sure they have the bacteria under control.*

She sat down in a chair and Cinnamon climbed up on her lap, nudging Janina's hand with her nose. Janina stroked her back. "Wow, you need a good brushing. I've been neglecting you lately, Toots. I think you'd better get used to it unless you can con David into doing the job." Cinnamon looked up at her with squinted eyes. Janina laughed. "Okay, so you don't believe me. You're probably right. I intend to keep our David very, very busy."

She leaned back in the chair and looked up at the ceiling. There was so much to do if she was going to be ready for the wedding on the twenty-third. Somehow, it still seemed part of a dream. She wanted to believe it would happen, but it was too good to be true. When David was there beside her, she was able to convince herself this wonderful dream was reality. But when he was gone... She shuddered. Thank God they didn't plan a long engagement. She couldn't survive the wait.

The doorbell rang. "David!" She dumped Cinnamon onto the floor and sprinted toward the front door. But even as she did, she knew it wasn't David. He had his own key.

She made an effort to compose herself as she slipped the latch and opened the door. It was the maintenance man.

"I came to spray for termites, Miss."

"Termites? I didn't know that was part of our maintenance package."

The man laughed. "Considering how much they

charge for upkeep on these here condos, they ought to spray every day."

"You've got a point there. Where's Joe? He usually does the spraying."

"Somebody said they had to scrub down the pool...you know...because of the malathion. They forgot to cover it last night and there's a layer of gook all over the top." He stepped inside, obviously in a hurry to get the job done. "I'll just be a minute. You'd better wait on the patio until I finish, then you can air the house out good."

"All right. Let me cover the fish tank and take the cat outside."

A few minutes later, he gave the all-clear and as Janina went inside, she heard the front door close. It took less than two seconds for her to realize that something was wrong. The odor of decaying licorice was so strong that she wanted to vomit.

"You bastard!" she said to the closed door. She didn't have to look out the window to know that hers was the only house he sprayed. Someone must have questioned Debbie to find out where she had been staying. It was a wise precaution, of course, but Janina bitterly resented the subterfuge.

It was about an hour later that Doug called from his father's house near Fremont. "Hey, listen, Janina. You guys aren't going to believe what just happened."

"They sprayed your dad's house for termites."

There was a long silence, then Doug laughed uneasily. "Well, yeah. How'd you guess?"

"They just left my place a little while ago and it smells to high heaven of rotten licorice."

"Yeah, I know. That's what made me catch on to what it really was they were doing. I guess we can't be too mad, though. It was probably a good idea to be on the safe side.''

''I know, but I don't have to like it.''

''Well, I just thought I'd tell you. I gotta go now. I promised Deb I'd be back up to see her tonight.''

''Maybe I'll see you up there, that is if David gets back in time.''

''You sound kind of down. Are you okay?''

''Sure. I just miss David, but he'll be back after a while. In the meantime, I've got to get this place aired out.''

They said goodbye and then Janina turned on the exhaust fan and started opening windows. David came home about forty-five minutes later.

''What the devil has been going on here?'' he demanded.

''You mean you don't like my new cologne?'' Janina asked dryly. ''We had a visit from our local branch of the committee to eradicate the fruit fly... only this time they called them termites. They sprayed Doug's father's house, too.''

David carefully placed on the kitchen table the box he had been carrying. ''Well, I suppose we should be glad that they're taking preventative measures. There's no telling how active the bacteria might be.''

''What, may I ask, do you have in the box?''

''You'd never guess in a million years.''

Janina walked all around it and pretended to study the large carton that nearly covered the top of the table. ''Perfume? I could use some right now.''

David grinned. ''Not even close.'' He pulled on a flap and opened the top, then extracted a portable video camera and handed it to Janina. ''Careful. This didn't come in a box of Cracker Jack.''

"It's heavy. How are you supposed to hold it?"

He moved around behind her, in close so that they were touching. Lifting the camera, he brought it to rest on her shoulder. "There. That leaves your hand free to adjust the focus and the exposure."

"Easy for you to say."

"It's not that difficult. I just took a quick course in video cameras from my friend Teddy Liederbach."

Janina looked surprised. "The cameraman from 'What to Do before the Doctor Comes'?"

David chuckled. "One and the same. He's still working for cable TV."

"Then this stuff belongs to him?"

"No. It's ours. I thought we might want to take home movies of our child's first step, and our wedding."

"Terrific idea, only I'd like it better if you put them in their proper order."

David leaned down and nuzzled her neck. "Hey, I like this, having your hands occupied so you can't fight back."

"As if I ever did! Stop that, David. I'm going to drop this thing. It must have cost a small fortune. Couldn't you have settled for a simple movie camera?"

"I can afford the best, love. Nothing's too good for our family." He took the camera from her and placed it carefully on the kitchen counter. Then, turning, he pulled Janina into his arms and kissed her with surprising passion.

She stepped back and suddenly noticed the look of suppressed excitement in his eyes. "David Madison, what are you up to?"

"Can't you guess?"

"I haven't the vaguest idea."

"If I remember correctly, you said you wanted to sit in on the special meeting of the city council tomorrow afternoon. Since they aren't likely to send you an engraved invitation, I thought the next best thing would be to watch it on film."

Janina felt a tremor of excitement run through her. "Dear God, David. Do you think we can actually film it?"

"Not we. I thought I'd drop in on them . . . maybe get there an hour or so ahead of time . . . so as not to embarrass them." He grinned. "They'll never even have to know I'm there until I tell them."

Janina was appalled. "Listen, honey. Aren't you letting this commando business get a little out of hand? They could send you to Siberia for less than that."

"Not if I get the film out of there before they get hold of it. They would be too afraid of compromising their position."

Janina's breath caught in her throat. "But what about the sound? That is only good for the picture, isn't it?"

David fished in the carton and brought out a square box. "*Voilà!* The recorder. All we have to do is slip in a cassette, connect the leads to the camera and we have synchronized audio and video."

She blew her cheeks out. "Are you really going to go through with this?"

"I'm going to give it a try."

"Then I'm going with you."

"Only if you agree to wait in the car."

"You've got to be kidding."

"Listen, Janina. I need somebody to get the cassette to a safe place after it's recorded."

"Well, it isn't going to be me. We can have a messenger service waiting outside while we're inside doing our thing. Or maybe even Doug."

David shook his head. "Better not get him involved. The messenger service is a good idea. We can pay them enough to make it worthwhile."

"Then we're really going through with this? Is it really worth the risk, David? After all, the bacteria seems to be under control. Wouldn't we be taking a chance when there is no longer the need?"

"The danger might be over for this time, Janina, but how about the next time someone out at Langtree gets careless? Next time it could be the whole town that's exposed, instead of a handful of people."

She sighed. "You're right, of course. I just needed to hear you say it. I only wish it was over so we could get on with our lives."

He cupped his hand around the back of her neck and bent to kiss her. "Nobody wishes it more than I do, love, but we don't have to wait until then to be together. We have the whole night ahead of us."

"It's not nearly long enough."

He grinned. "I could think of a very clever remark, but it would only waste more time."

He saw her rubbing the back of her neck. "What say I give you one of Dr. Madison's special back rubs?"

"Sounds terrific."

He led her into the bedroom and she put on her dressing gown, while David pawed through the bathroom cabinet for a bottle of lotion and found one with a faint floral fragrance. "This should do it," he said. He warmed the lotion for a moment between the palms of his hands, then began to massage her back in slow, measured circles. He carefully avoided the sexual areas of her body, but instead of lessening the feeling of sensuality, it served to increase it. Janina was being drawn into a maelstrom of sensations that spun her senses around and sent them whirling into a torrent of desire.

"Asleep?" he asked, teasing.

"I may never wake up again." Her voice sounded drugged with pleasure.

"That boring, huh? Then maybe this will get your attention." He turned her over and anointed her neck and shoulders in soft, wispy strokes. Then he moved lower, rolling the lotion softly over her breasts and rib cage with infinite tenderness.

Janina moaned. "This is torture. You know that, don't you, David?"

"I'm rather enjoying it."

"Wait till we see how you stand up under the same treatment."

"I can hardly wait."

She reached up and, grabbing his ears in her fingers, gently pulled him down until her mouth found his. "I hope you're not tired, David, because you're not going to get very much sleep tonight."

He laughed. "Speaking of torture!"

Chapter Eleven

Janina's internal alarm system had not reprogrammed itself to her new life-style of being unemployed. Promptly at 6:00 A.M., she awoke and started to get up until she felt David's tempting warmth in the bed next to her. She smiled and he opened his eyes.

"What's the matter? Was I snoring?"

"Well, besides that...I was just thinking about the adage that every cloud has a silver lining. But this one is better. It's pure gold."

He yawned. "How so?"

"I may be on disciplinary suspension, but I don't really feel like I'm being punished when I wake up to find you in my bed and realize that we can spend the whole day together."

"On the other hand, it doesn't seem right for you just to lie there wasting your time."

"Oh? What do you suggest?"

"Under other circumstances, I might have suggested that you bring me breakfast in bed, but I'm afraid it would be my last meal."

"David! I'm warning you."

"So just to keep you active..." He rolled over against her and put his arm under her head. They focused on each other's eyes, saying nothing, but communicating as easily as if their thoughts were engraved in bronze. What they sensed went far beyond the physical hunger that had driven them together. Janina gloried in the love she saw written in the dark-blue depths of David's eyes. David said a prayer of gratitude that the love he so freely gave was returned in kind. He had never felt so completely satisfied, so lovingly attuned to another human being.

"I love you, Janina Scott," he said when he could stand the silence no longer.

"And I love you, David Madison. More than I love life."

He kissed her forehead, holding her in his arms as if the moment could last forever. It occurred to David that making love again would be the icing on the cake, but he held back. The mood was too precious to risk losing. A short time later they both drifted off to sleep, still wrapped in the warm cocoon of their love.

Just after ten that morning, they went to the hospital to see Debbie and to look in on Doug's father. Both were doing well. Debbie said that her doctor was going to release her the next day. Mr. Fairfax would remain yet another week if all went well.

As they were leaving the hospital parking lot, Janina looked over at David with a peculiar expression in her eyes. He looked back at the line of traffic waiting at the light.

"All right, love. What's bothering you?"

"I...I just can't make myself believe this isn't all a dream. Are we really getting married on the twenty-third?"

"We have to now, Jan. I've already made arrangements for the ceremony to take place at your family church. I know that's the bride's prerogative to take care of those things, but I thought you would be pleased if I handled them. Besides, it's just insurance on my part... to make sure you won't change your mind.''

Janina brushed her hand along his leg as he compressed the brake pedal. ''Your chances of getting away from me now, my friend, are extremely remote. Of course, after today we may be spending the rest of our short engagement in separate cells in the county jail but—''

''Don't even think that way. We're going to bring this off. I know we are. Once it's over, there's nothing to stand in the way of our getting married.''

''Have you heard from your father yet?''

''Not yet, but we will. Stop worrying, Jan. He's going to love you.''

''I hope so. He's the only family you have for now and I want him to be happy about our marriage. I'm just glad he isn't around here to blame me for turning you into a commando.''

David grinned. ''You don't know my dad. He's conservative, but he admires people who have the courage to stand up for what they believe.''

''Right now I'm beginning to run a little short of courage.'' She looked at her watch. ''We don't have that much time if we plan to get into city hall by twelve-thirty. What about the guard? Won't he try to stop us?''

''He goes on lunch break at twelve-fifteen. He eats at his desk, but he takes a few minutes out to get coffee from the machine and go to the john. That leaves us just enough time to get our equipment into the projection booth without being seen.''

''You have it all planned out, don't you?''

''I hope so, love. I truly hope so.''

She laughed shakily. "Do we wear our black jeans and turtleneck sweaters again?"

"No. The uniform of the day is blue suits. You know...so we'll blend into the background along with the mayor and the other VIPs."

"Right. I'll do my best."

She took him literally, putting on a dark-blue suit with an ivory ruffled blouse. It made her look slimmer and very capable, she thought. David thought it made her look sexy.

He whistled. "No way are you going to fade into the background, lady." His gaze traveled down her hips to her long, elegant legs. "Something tells me you should have worn your running shoes."

Janina looked startled. "Will they chase us?"

"Not us, dummy. You." He leered at her as if she were a ripe plum waiting to be plucked.

"Stop it, David. I'm too nervous to keep up with your wild sense of humor." She saw that he, too, was wearing navy. The suit and the beige shirt with its tiny blue trefoils fit him as if they were tailor-made. They probably were.

He put his arm across her shoulder and kissed her cheek. "Not too late to change your mind, love. I can do it alone."

"Over my dead body." She shot a look at him and then smiled weakly. "Oh, I'm sorry I said that."

He grinned. "Ready to go?"

"No...but lead the way."

"Why the big handbag? Isn't it a little out of character?"

"Maybe. I know it doesn't quite go with the suit, but it's my security blanket. My good-luck purse. Isn't it all right?"

He shrugged. "It doesn't matter to me."

They had discussed at length how to carry the camera and recorder into city hall. For a while they considered taking it in plain view, but finally agreed that was tempting fate. The final decision was to carry it in the box with large, hand-lettered words on the side: Budget Committee Reports, 1979–1983. Janina carried a steno pad in plain view of anyone who chanced to look.

There was a motley assortment of cars in the lot next to city hall. Just enough to give them a comfortable feeling of anonymity.

"Now, if we pass anyone," David said, "keep up a low, running conversation about reports or schedules so that we don't have to look directly at them. If we avoid eye contact, they'll be less likely to remember us or to think about what we're doing there."

He shoved the door of the Mercedes shut with his foot. Janina noticed that he hadn't locked the doors. Odd. *My God,* she thought. *Does he think we might have to make a run for it?* She wasn't about to ask him, but the thought nagged at her and the perspiration began to bead across the bridge of her nose.

Instead of going around to the front entrance, David led the way toward a door at the rear of the building, just a few feet from where he parked. Janina expected it to be locked, but miraculously, it was open. She held it while David preceded her, then turned left at the first corridor. The door closed with a swoosh that seemed to echo through the marble silence. She followed close behind David, painfully aware of the click her heels made against the highly polished floor.

A door opened and a woman came toward them. Janina drew a strangled breath. "I think you'll find the reports are in order. We checked back through seventy-nine and cataloged them by day, date and time into the proper sequences, then fed them into the computer and made forty-two copies of the readouts, which we mailed in triplicate to the head office.'' The woman disappeared into another room with hardly a glance in their direction.

"What'd I say?" Janina asked breathlessly.

"Beats me, but I think it worked." He nodded toward a small door at the end of the hallway. "That should be it."

"Are you sure?"

He gave her a look. "No. If you must know the truth. But it's about the way Teddy described it. Open the door for me."

She turned the knob. "I can't, David. It's locked." Her eyes were wide with desperation.

"Okay. Don't panic. Have you got a credit card?"

She dug deeply into her bag for her wallet. With shaking fingers, she pulled the card out of its enclosure then shoved it between the door and the frame as she turned the knob. "My God, it worked. I got it unlocked."

"Move it, will you, love? Let's get in and close the door before someone else discovers how smart you are."

She nearly jumped at his command. The room was dark as she closed the door after them. "I think I'm getting claustrophobia," she whispered. "It's so dark in here."

"Well, turn on the light."

"Won't somebody see it?" She felt along the wall for the switch.

"I doubt it. This is a projection booth. There aren't any windows. That's better," he said as she flipped on the switch. "Yup. It's just like Teddy described it.

There's the camera mount. Over here's the connector for the recorder. Now all we have to do is make certain that the mikes are turned on.''

"I thought we'd be able to see what's going on at the meeting.''

"Only through the viewfinder on the camera. They can't see us, either.''

"Thank heaven for that. Can they hear us, though?''

"I hope not. We'll have to talk very quietly, just in case. After we turn on the microphones, we'd better lock the door to the hall and the one going into the council room, just in case they decide to check out the projection booth.''

Janina peeked through the camera aperture and saw that the council room was empty. She opened the door and the room, richly paneled and carpeted, reminded her of the courthouse the two times she sat on a jury. It wasn't reassuring.

"Can you turn on the microphone switches?'' David asked.

"I'll try." She moved toward the long table where the members of the council, along with the others who were invited, would be seated. There were only a few microphones. Not nearly enough to go around.

Janina worried about it. "David, how are we going to hear what everyone says?''

"We'll have to use full volume. They won't be making any effort to use the mikes, so we'll have to compensate for that and hope it picks up everything.''

"Are we going to try it out in advance?''

"I thought about it, but I'm afraid to take the chance. We'll just have to wing it.''

Janina locked the doors and then sat down to watch

David mount and adjust the lens to give a full view of the table. Only one or two of those present would have their backs to the camera.

Janina started to ask David about the speaker system when he motioned her to be quiet. Holding her breath, she got up to stand beside him.

He pulled her close and whispered in her ear. "A woman just came in with glasses and a pitcher of ice water." They stood motionless for what seemed like an excruciatingly long time as she moved deliberately around the table, adjusting the chairs, then placing an empty water glass and an ashtray a prescribed number of inches from the edge of the table.

David slowly let out his breath and visibly relaxed. "It's all clear. She's gone now."

Janina looked at her watch. "We still have over a half-hour to wait. I wish we could get this over with."

David smiled over at her. "It's going better than I could have imagined. Everything is exactly as Teddy said it would be."

"That's what worries me. I'd rather have things go wrong now instead of later when we run the danger of getting caught. If somebody comes in here—"

"They can't, love. You locked the door."

Janina gave him a cool look. "Are you going to pretend I'm the only one who has a credit card?"

"No. But who else has your special talents?"

"It's the first time I ever tried that, David. I saw it done on television."

"Likely story."

"You're going to tease me once too often, Buster."

He grinned wickedly and patted her bottom. "I'll give you a chance to get even tonight."

"That is if the matron will let you into my cell."

David moved back to the table and flexed his back and neck muscles. *He's not as calm as he pretends,* Janina thought.

He moved her handbag as he leaned against the edge of the table. "What do you have inside there, anyway, a salami?"

"I thought we might get hungry."

"You're crazy, Jan."

"It's the company I keep."

"Did I ever tell you I love you?"

"Tell me again."

"I love you, Nina."

Her eyes suddenly misted. "Oh, David. I love you, too."

He reached for her hands and pressed them between his large palms and they stood there looking at each other as if they alone existed in the world. Reluctantly he let her go and looked at his watch.

"They should start coming in any minute now." He frowned in concentration. "I'm going to turn the camera on now to let it warm up and so they'll be accustomed to the noise if it can be heard out there."

Janina looked at the recorder and wondered what the switches were for. "I was just wondering, David. Aren't the table microphones intended to amplify the sound to the auditorium? Won't the members be able to tell that the speakers are turned on?"

He swore softly. "You're right. I had forgotten all about that. I remember now that Teddy said something about switching the sound from the speakers to the recorder." He moved quickly toward the box and scanned the switches. "Here. This is the one." He flipped it to the left and slowly let out his breath. "My God, we nearly blew the whole ball game." He looked around the room to see if everything else was in order. "I guess we'd better turn off the lights just as an extra measure of safety, and let's keep our voices down."

Janina had discovered a small opening through which she could view the proceedings in the outer room. Quickly she put her hand on his arm and touched a finger to her lips. The members had begun to arrive.

The camera stuttered ominously for a brief moment then settled into a faint hum that was barely audible in the small room. Janina's heart thudded against her rib cage and she held on to the edge of the table to steady herself. David looked so calm, so capable, as he bent to direct the camera to a new angle. Janina swallowed with difficulty, wishing she had a drink of water to ease her throat.

Her nerves were stripped bare, sensitive to the least sound, the most innocuous glance toward the projection room. She felt the blood rush through her body at an incredible rate. Her breath came fast and short.

Steady there, she cautioned herself. *It's going to be over in a little while and we'll have all the proof we need to keep Langtree under control.*

David looked over at her and smiled reassuringly. She forced a smile in return, hoping, as she did, that David wouldn't know how scared she was.

The sound of voices from the council room was just barely audible. Janina pressed her nose against the wall and stared through the tiny opening. "It looks like about eighteen men. That's the editor of the *Evening Sentinel*, wearing the green tie, and beside him on the left is the city attorney. I don't know who the man next to him is."

David nodded, whispering. "And there's our friend Randolph Baker from the hospital."

And my dear Dr. Morrison, she thought dryly. *No wonder he got so ticked when I asked to see his patient charts. Thank God I broke off with him before things got serious.* Out loud she said, "I wonder who that is at the head of the table."

"I'd be willing to bet it's one of the Langtree clan and that's probably his retinue of attorneys on his right. Wait. He's calling the meeting to order."

Janina could just barely hear what was being said. It was the Langtree man at the head of the table who seemed to be in charge. His voice was steady and firm, leaving no doubt as to his position of authority.

"Gentlemen, we all know why we are here. I fervently hope that this will be our last meeting, and I am confident that it will be. Everything is pretty well under control... and thanks to each of you for your strict attention to details, we have prevented the situation from spilling over into the community in general." He shot a glance toward the man at his right. "I'm sure Lyle will agree that from a legal standpoint we have taken enough precautions to prevent any untoward repercussions."

The newspaper editor cleared his throat. "Surely, Mr. Langtree, you aren't going to overlook the death of one of the victims or even the incident of the stolen tr—" He was interrupted before he could finish by lawyers from both sides of the table. One of them was red-faced as he spoke.

"I thought we agreed to avoid specifics. Even at this stage of the game, we can't afford to be careless."

"Sorry." The editor looked properly contrite. "But I think you know to what I'm referring. The... confiscation could easily become a police matter."

The police chief spoke up. "No need to worry on that

score. As soon as the lab gives us the all-clear, we will see that the item in question is returned in good condition.''

Randolph Baker nervously tapped the table with his fingertips. ''But what we have here is much more involved than a simple theft and its repercussions. There are a number of families who have incurred staggering expenses, not to mention the pain some people had to face. Granted, the situation is now under control, but does that cancel out the debt and does it mean that you've put an end to your... uh, experimentation?''

Mr. Langtree's well-oiled voice floated across the room like a drop of mercury on a glass platter. ''Research, Randolph. Not experiments. Semantics, I admit, but under the circumstances we want to avoid confusion.''

He fingered a heavy gold cuff link and there was a momentary pause in the conversation. At that moment David's digital watch beeped twice to mark the hour. Janina let out a yelp of surprise. The men at the table suddenly stopped moving and the silence was like a living entity. Janina could hear her own heartbeat.

''What was that?'' Randolph Baker demanded, looking around.

Mayor Allen laughed shortly. ''It's nothing. Just this damned watch of mine. It beeps on the hour, every hour. Most of the time I don't hear it and I forgot about it until now.''

Langtree laughed jovially. ''Would you say we're all a little inclined to look over our shoulders these days?''

The police chief got up. ''Just the same, I think I'll check out the entrances.'' He tried the main door to the council room, then came toward the projection room, passing out of camera range as he approached the door. Janina and David froze in position as they saw the doorknob turn.

"Seems to be secure." The chief's voice was frighteningly loud at that close range. He jiggled the knob several times. "Does anyone here have a key?"

Someone laughed. "Since when did you need a key, Mike?"

"You know I'd never break the law, Joe. They just do things like that in the movies."

Laughter reverberated around the room. Everyone in town knew that the police chief interpreted the law to his advantage. It was only the fact that crime had decreased considerably since he took office that he was allowed such latitude. The thought scared the wits out of Janina. If he unlocked the door, she and David were in real trouble.

But apparently the police chief decided the locked door posed no threat, because the conversation resumed. The man from Langtree Labs was responding to an earlier question by Randolph Baker.

"Surely, Mr. Baker, you can't expect Langtree Industries to pay reparations? As to the research. My good man, half the people in this town owe their existence to the fact that we've kept the town alive throughout the recession. We must continue to grow, to explore new fields. The future of medicine lies with the type of studies we carry on out at Langtree Labs and we intend to make certain that Willowbrook will be one of the leading research centers in the world. Do you have any idea what that means to a young community such as this?"

It was plain to see that the mayor was impressed. He wasn't the only one. Randolph Baker, now properly chastised, slumped in his chair. "I suppose we have to make a certain number of sacrifices, but we will have to have some assurance that. . ."

He continued to ramble on. Janina wanted to strangle him. She touched David's arm. "They aren't saying a thing," she whispered. "This isn't helping a bit."

Even in the dim light Janina could see that David's face was grim. "I know it. I'm afraid they outsmarted us. I thought surely they'd say something that would incriminate them."

"How much more tape do you have?"

"Enough. They sound like they're getting ready to wind it up, anyway."

"We can't let them go until we get something."

David's heart was wrenched by the disappointment in her voice. "Face it, love. We gave it our best shot. I really don't know what else we can do."

Janina was torn by indecision. Then she spread her hands in a helpless gesture and turned her head to look again through the peephole.

After the key incident, the mood in the council room lightened considerably. Someone said something in a low voice, and the man next to the police chief nudged him playfully in the ribs. His toothy grin would have made his dentist proud.

Langtree flattened his palms on the table and appeared to be ready to leave. "Gentlemen, if there is nothing else I think we may consider the incident closed. I want to thank each one of you again for your cooperation. By the way, I'm having a little weekend party at my ranch out in the valley and I would. . ." His voice diminished to nothing as Janina moved away from the wall.

"Keep the camera rolling, David, until the last man leaves the room."

"Sure," he said, without looking up.

Janina was angry. She hadn't felt such anger since she was told her perfect examination paper in college would not be counted because a few people had cheated on the test. That time she had smothered her anger, but this time was different. She was determined to do something.

Reaching down into her bulky handbag she pulled out the black rubber-covered thermos bottle she had taken on the picnic the day she and David were stopped by the motorcycle cops. Her hands had stopped trembling. Now that she had made up her mind to go through with it, she was beyond fear.

David, intent on operating the camera, was unaware of what she was doing. He looked up as she opened the door to the council room, but he was too late to stop her. She relocked the door and stepped into the chambers, much to the obvious shock of the eighteen men present.

"Gentlemen, please stay where you are." She didn't have to tell them. Those who started to get up simply dropped into their chairs.

"Miss Scott, what the devil are you doing here?" Randolph Baker demanded.

"You know this woman?" the man from Langtree asked.

"She's the one we've been talking about. Patient coordinator at the hospital until I had her replaced."

The editor stared wide-eyed. "And she's the one who provided the sample of the bactericide...and wanted us to print the article in the *Sentinel*."

Janina, clutching the thermos in front of her as if

afraid it would fall, approached slowly. Mr. Langtree studied her with measured gaze.

"You've been a busy little lady, my dear. Unfortunately for you, you are trespassing on a private meeting. The police chief, here, could have you arrested."

Janina didn't speak because her nerve had about spent itself. Then Langtree continued.

"As it is, I'm sure the chief will want to question you immediately about what you're doing here."

The chief started to get up and Janina was jolted into action.

"Sit down. All of you. If one of you comes toward me, I'll dump the contents of this container all over the room."

"Just what is it, a bomb?" someone demanded.

Janina drew a deep breath as she turned to the police chief. "If you bothered to check the police reports, you may remember that I was seen a few days ago near the Langtree property. Two motorcycle policemen stopped me and a friend of mine while we were horseback riding along the fence bordering the laboratory grounds." She looked down at the thermos and gingerly lifted it in both hands, to the height of her chest. "The report may have mentioned that we carried a canister in the saddlebag. Does that sound familiar?"

The police chief nodded. "I had a gut feeling the two of you had actually broken into the lab. After reading the report, I wondered if my officers had made a serious mistake in judgment by letting you go free. Now I know."

The men closest to her had begun to lean away from her, but not one dared move out of his chair. She had positioned herself so that her back was off-center to the camera and everyone was in clear view of the lens.

Mr. Langtree's voice was harsh. "Just what is it you want from us, Miss Scott?"

"The truth, for a starter. I want you to tell me about the bacteria that got loose at the lab and what you plan to do about it."

There was a general gasp of astonishment, but Langtree's voice outweighed them. "I haven't the slightest idea what you're talking about."

Randolph Baker spoke wearily. "Oh, for heaven's sake, stop playing games. She knows everything. We were fools to think we could cover it up indefinitely. Some of the doctors who weren't in on it began to suspect when they saw traces of the mutant bacteria on some of the slides. You can't hide something like that for long. My God, we had a death at the hospital. Doesn't that mean anything to you men?"

Janina was surprised by his support. She gathered her courage around her like a cloak. "There are quite a number of people who know about this. It's not going to go away, even if you have the bacteria under control. We aren't going to let something like this happen again. This time it stopped short of epidemic. Next time it might become pandemic."

Mr. Langtree appeared to have lost some of his stuffing. He leaned back against the chair and rested his arms across his chest, making a pyramid of his fingers as he tapped them together. "I don't think you realize how important this research is to the field of medicine, Miss Scott. Janina, isn't it? I'm told you're a trained professional. Surely it must mean something to you that we are attempting to isolate a bacteria that can mean the end to several serious afflictions. This mutant bacteria that was revealed during our experiments proved to be unfriendly and, through an unforeseen accident, it temporarily got away form us. But those things happen. With continued research, we may find that this very same bacteria may be of great value to the medical world.''

"It's not the experiments I object to, Mr. Langtree. It's your lack of safety precautions. Your scientists should have been aware from the beginning that the particular filters used in the air-conditioning system were not adequate to permit isolation of certain strains of bacteria and viruses. I also object to your lack of concern for the community, in that you faked an invasion of the fruit fly in order to cover up the fact that the bacteria got loose.''

"The fruit fly was a convenient means to an end, and I resent the criticism, Miss Scott.''

"Not nearly as much as I resent my sister and my friends having to suffer the pain of acute pancreatitis when treatment with gamma globulin could have prevented it.''

He looked shocked. "May I ask how you came to that information?''

"By process of elimination. It was quite obvious that select groups of people appeared to be immune to the disease. Gamma globulin was the one thing they all had in common.''

"Remarkable. It was only this morning that my scientists arrived at the same conclusion.''

"That's my point, Mr. Langtree. If you had reported the breach of safety to the Department of Immunology, more people would have been involved in finding a preventative medicine.''

"And we could also have had panic in the streets,

my dear.'' He smiled warmly. "Now, why don't you just hand over that canister and let us take care of it from here on?"

"I'm afraid I'm not quite ready to do that, Mr. Langtree."

His voice became harsh. "Then we shall have to take it away from you, won't we?"

Several men started to rise at once. With a calm that belied the shaking inside her, Janina held the thermos bottle out in front of her and slowly began to unscrew the lid. It grated ominously and they sat down quickly.

"All right, Miss Scott. What is it you want from us?"

"To begin with, I want it in writing that Langtree Labs will confine its experiments, inside the city limits of Willowbrook, to the testing of chemical- or plant-based medical products. I believe this is already controlled by a city ordinance." She saw several heads nod in agreement. "In addition, I want a financial settlement made to those who have become ill from contact with the bacteria."

"I suppose we could do that."

"And in addition, I want the air-conditioning truck that belongs to Mr. Fairfax returned as soon as it is decontaminated."

A soft chuckle rippled around the room. Mr. Langtree echoed the smile. "If I agree to those things, will you hand over the canister?"

"If you'll give your word."

"Then you have it. I agree to the terms."

"And you also admit to the cover-up?"

"I do."

Holding the thermos bottle carefully with both hands in front of her, Janina walked slowly toward the table. "All right. Since I have your word, I'll stand by mine."

The men moved away from her in obvious fear of contamination, but Mr. Langtree reached for the canister with a white handkerchief wrapped around his hand, then as if on second thought, told her to put it on the table and step away from it.

"Now then, Miss Scott," he said. "You may consider yourself under arrest."

A shock went through Janina as surely as if she had stuck her finger in an electric-light socket. She couldn't speak, but it didn't matter. Mr. Langtree gave her no opportunity. He spoke harshly.

"As for our little agreement, I feel no obligation to follow through, inasmuch as my promise was obtained under duress."

Randolph Baker leaned forward. "Mr. Langtree, I wonder if perhaps we should discuss this further before you do anything we might regret. With all due respect, sir. Miss Scott is a highly capable individual with a rather wide range of acquaintances because of her particular work at the hospital. If you have her arrested, the matter will quickly become common knowledge."

There was a murmur of agreement among the men, but Langtree remained firm. "She's a troublemaker, that's all. I know how to deal with people like her." He grabbed her arm and turned to the chief of police. "Mike, this is your job. See that it gets done."

The chief rose slowly from his chair and approached Janina. He looked slightly embarrassed. "I'm sorry, Miss Scott." He shrugged and extracted a card from his breast pocket. "It's my duty to inform you that anything you say may be held against you."

Chapter Twelve

Somewhere in the back of her mind, Janina was dimly aware that she was being read her rights by the head of Willowbrook's police department. The functioning part of her brain was convinced that it all had to be part of a bad dream. An ugly silence filled the room, an underlying current of dissent among the men gathered around the conference table. The anger appeared to be directed at Mr. Langtree, but apparently no one man had the courage to face him down. The police chief finished reading Janina her rights and stuffed the card into his pocket.

He scanned the table. "Would one of you step outside and ask my deputy to come in?"

No one rose, but at that moment the door to the projection room opened and David stood there casually leaning against the door frame.

"I wouldn't advise that, Chief, unless you want this farce spread over the entire country. I just completed filming the entire meeting from the moment you all arrived here at one-thirty and I have already dispatched a videocassette to my attorney."

Langtree jumped up from the table. "I don't believe it. Where's the camera?"

David moved gracefully aside and allowed him to enter the projection booth. "You see? Camera, recorder. . . everything we needed to capture the sight and the sound of the whole meeting."

Langtree studied the camera. "It's still running. You didn't take out the cassette."

"That's a second one. I believe in hedging my bets, but I assure you, Mr. Langtree, there was enough material on the first tape to incriminate every one of you."

Langtree turned angrily and strode back to the table. "Are we going to let him get away with this? It's blackmail. Dammit, that's illegal."

The mayor nodded. "Actually, sir, what we are doing here is also illegal. Willowbrook has always taken great pride in its 'government in the sunshine' law. Legally, we can't meet like this without a public statement. With all due respect, I think it's time we reconsidered our course of action."

Heads nodded agreement and the room came alive with feelings that had been too long held in check. The chief patted Janina's arm and went back to his chair. She slowly let out her breath.

With David and Janina standing there listening, the council agreed to hold to their promise to restrict Langtree's experiments and to award a settlement to those who had been injured by the bacteria. It was also ordered that the truck would be returned to Doug as soon as it was properly decontaminated.

But Langtree wasn't so easily placated. "Since I seem to have no choice, I will have to agree to everything you said, but that isn't the end of it." He stood up with his hands flat on the table, his face white with rage. "Chief Wilson, I want you to arrest Miss Scott for theft of Langtree property."

"Oh, come on, Alfred." The chief sighed. "Haven't we done enough to this young woman and her family?"

"I gave an order and I expect it to be carried out. Either that or I plan to start moving Langtree Industries out of town the moment our leases expire."

The police chief looked haggard, but he got up and walked back toward Janina. "I'm really sorry about this, but under the circumstances I have no choice. You all but admitted the theft of the bacteria and the evidence is right here in front of us."

Janina pressed her hands together in front of her and took a deep breath. "May I ask exactly what I'm being accused of?"

Langtree laughed sharply, then jabbed his finger at the canister. "Theft of confidential materials from Langtree Laboratories."

Janina picked up the thermos bottle. "You mean this?" Before anyone knew what she was doing, she unscrewed the cap and took a long drink.

There was a gasp of surprise, but the outburst turned to shock as she coughed harshly and started to choke. No one moved, not even Dr. Morrison, who was seated close to where she was standing. She coughed again and tried to clear her throat. By this time a number of men got up and would have come to her aid but she shook her head and motioned them away.

David looked at her intently for an instant then casually pounded her on the back.

"Don't panic, anyone. Janina makes lousy coffee. Even she can't stand to drink it."

When she caught her breath and managed to convince the men that David was telling the truth, they all looked chagrined and began talking among themselves. Chief Wilson's eyebrows lifted.

"Well, sir. Unless the coffee is considered confidential material, we don't seem to have much of a case against Miss Scott."

There was a rumble of laughter, and Mr. Langtree banged on the table to restore order. A discussion followed, concerning what measures were to be taken to set things right. David and Janina agreed that nothing was to be gained by alerting the public to the cover-up now that the bactericide had brought the emergency under control.

Mr. Langtree, seeing that everyone had turned against him, agreed to pay a settlement and to move that particular branch of the laboratories to a remote piece of property farther up into the foothills. Everyone was relieved.

The meeting disintegrated after that. David collected the camera equipment and they left the building in high spirits.

"Okay, smarty," Janina asked the minute they closed the doors of the Mercedes. "How did you know it was coffee in the thermos bottle?"

"Just a lucky guess. You were really taking a chance with them, you know. It's lucky they didn't shoot you on the spot."

"Come on, David. This is Willowbrook, not some foreign country. Those men, except for Mr. Langtree maybe, are just people like you and me. They wanted to put an end to the cover-up just as much as we did. Didn't you notice how Randolph Baker mellowed once he saw the way things were turning out?"

"Only because he came to realize where the power lies. You watch. Before the week is out, he's going to be calling you back to work."

She shook her head. "Not one chance in a million.

He'll wait for me to come begging, and I don't do that. I wish he would reinstate me, though. There are a lot of loose ends I'd like to tie up before I leave Willowbrook.''

"Baker isn't stupid.''

"Never that. I really think he's insecure. Randolph was frightened and didn't see any way out of the situation except to do what Mr. Langtree ordered.''

He reached over and tousled her hair. "I think you're being extremely generous, but since I happen to be first in line to benefit from your overdeveloped sense of fairness, how can I complain?''

She pulled his hand down to her mouth and pressed a kiss into his palm. "I'm glad you were there, David.''

"I'll always be there when you need me.'' He reached over and patted the space next to him. She didn't need a second invitation.

They had been home less than an hour when Randolph Baker called. His voice was friendly. No mention was made of the incident at city hall.

"Now, Janina. The reason I'm calling, since everything seems to be getting back to normal I want you to report to work tomorrow morning as usual. I assume you can do that?''

"Why, yes, I imagine so.''

"Very well, we'll expect you then. Goodbye.''

He hung up before she had a chance to thank him for calling. Janina slowly replaced the receiver. "You'll never guess what that was about.''

"Randolph Baker asking you to come back to work?''

"Yes. Come on, David. Darn you anyway. He must have said something to you. I know you're not *that* clever.''

"What a way to talk to your future husband."

"Well...maybe you are clever at that." She wrapped her arms around his waist. "You proposed to me, didn't you? With all of Sunnyvale, Willowbrook and San Jose looking on?"

"Smartest thing I ever did. So what about work? Are you going to start in again?"

Janina pushed her hair away from her face. "I really should, much as I hate to be away from you. I want to clean up my files and write some reports in order to make a smooth transition for my replacement."

"There isn't much time until the twenty-third."

"I know. But sometimes it seems like forever."

"My thoughts exactly," he said, stroking her fingers.

They heard the cat-door bell sound and Cinnamon wandered into the house looking very pleased with herself. She stopped in the doorway and waited as a scraggly-looking black tomcat came up behind her.

"Well, what have we here?" David laughed. "Look who's been doing the town."

Janina jumped up. "How did he get in here? I thought Cinnamon was the only one who could get in the door."

"Looks like she gave him the combination."

Janina open the door and shooed him out. "Whew! He must be the cat from the fish market down the street. I can't say much for her taste in friends."

"Don't worry. She'll forget all about him once we get to San Diego." Cinnamon gave them a smug look of satisfaction and headed toward the chow line.

While Janina changed into a pale-blue silky-looking dress, David made reservations for an early dinner. On the way they stopped in the hospital to see Debbie and

Mr. Fairfax. Debbie was restless about having to stay in the hospital for another night, until Doug arrived to see her. There was no doubt in Janina's mind that Debbie was in love with Doug.

When a nurse came to take her temperature, Janina and David took Doug out into the corridor and told him what had taken place that afternoon. He was overwhelmed.

"So it's finally over," he said, shaking his head. "I still can't believe it really happened."

"You're not alone," Janina agreed. "I'll call you when they return your truck, but there's no hurry about returning my car."

He thanked them and went back inside to be with Debbie.

After a leisurely dinner in a candlelit restaurant, David and Janina went home. There were no spray planes that night. The announcer gave full credit to an alert Department of Agriculture for its aggressive campaign against the fruit fly.

WHEN SHE ARRIVED at her office the following morning, Janina was greeted with looks of surprise. It occurred to her that no one would ever understand the real reason for her return. Probably Randolph Baker would get the credit for being generous. She sighed. As long as everything turned out well, that was all that mattered. In just a few short days she'd be leaving.

One thing, though. She had been missed. There was a long list of messages from staff and patients who were complaining about the way various procedures had been handled. Apparently, the rumors were true. Freddie Guilford was not working out as her replacement. She wasn't surprised. The man lacked the courage to stand up to anyone. He was a yes man. The job needed someone who was strong enough to face down administration and nursing staff as well as people from insurance companies and government agencies.

There was another complaint about Nurse O'Connor, in Physical Therapy. Janina had pushed that problem to the back of her mind, but now it needed attention. She lifted the telephone and dialed the operator. "Would you page Mrs. O'Connor, Physical Therapy, and ask her to come to my office as soon as possible?"

Once it was done, Janina didn't know how she was going to handle it. O'Connor needed the job desperately, but she was clearly unable to manage the hard physical labor required to work with handicapped patients. She was a strong-minded woman, and intelligent. A valuable employee under other circumstances, one that personnel would not want to let go though they would be forced to do so if no one intervened.

There was no time to belabor the decision. O'Connor arrived a few minutes later. She was a reasonably attractive woman. Janina was impressed with her air of confidence when she surely must have guessed that she was in trouble.

"Would you like a cup of coffee?" Janina asked.

"Tea, if you have it, please."

Janina rinsed the pot and filled it with hot water. While she was waiting for the tea to brew she broached the subject.

"You must know, Joyce, that there have been quite a number of complaints about your attitude. Do you want to tell me about it?"

"I do the best I can, Miss Scott."

"I realize that the work is physically demanding." She hesitated. "You've been in considerable pain, haven't you?"

"How did you know?" she asked, surprised, then immediately tried to cover. "It's nothing. I can handle it."

"I know you've been trying. But the pain is affecting your attitude toward your patients."

"Please. I'll do better. I can't lose this job. I have children to take care of. There's no one else but me to look out for them."

"I see by your résumé that you also have training in social work. Have you considered moving into that branch of health care?"

"I've thought about it quite a bit. I like people and get along with them very well. . .at least I used to before I came under so much pressure to keep my job. The problem is one of logistics. I need set hours and I can't be running all over town the way most social workers have to, because I have to be available in case my children need me."

"If I can find another position for you, would you consider taking it?"

O'Connor's eyes filled with tears. "Is there a chance that might happen? If there is, I'd be forever grateful."

"I'll certainly do my best."

When she left, O'Connor was smiling for the first time in weeks.

Janina was smiling, too. In one short interview she knew that she had found her replacement. It was perfect. If O'Connor lacked a certain degree of finesse, it was something she could acquire in time. She was tough, but she was also quite cordial when she wasn't in pain. The pain would disappear once there was an end to the heavy lifting. The touch of belligerence would go once O'Connor realized her job was not in jeopardy and the income she needed to support her family was safe.

Janina stopped in to see Randolph Baker later that afternoon and submitted her resignation. He pretended to be disappointed, but there really had never been a close relationship between them. His last attempt to make up for his earlier treatment of Janina was to offer the job as her replacement to Nurse O'Connor, but he insisted the offer come directly from him. Janina didn't care in the least. All that mattered was that O'Connor's job was safe and that the hospital would benefit from it.

Late that afternoon, as she climbed the stairway to the third floor West to have coffee with Casey, Janina was brimming with happiness.

Casey looked at her with undisguised amazement. "I told them you'd get the best of Randy Baker, but I didn't think you'd be back this soon. What happened? Did you get the creep fired?"

Janina laughed. "You might say we reached a compromise."

"Too bad. I liked it better my way. Well, what happened about the malathion thing? I listened to the TV all last night and they never once mentioned a different kind of spray like you said they would. I guess you made a mistake, huh?"

Janina smiled. "It wouldn't be my first."

Casey chewed thoughtfully on a doughnut and studied Janina's face. "Something happened, didn't it? But you can't talk about it. Right?"

"It's over now, and the less said about it the better. I have to admit, though, that Mr. Baker has a few good qualities that I overlooked before."

Casey snorted. "Now, that's like putting ice cream on a toad pie."

Janina laughed and gave her a hug. "You're so good for me, Case. I'm going to miss you."

When Janina got home from work that evening, David had dinner ready to pop under the broiler. He looked as if he were holding something back.

"All right, David. I know that look in your eyes and I also know that we're having lobster for dinner. What's up?"

"Good news. A cable just arrived from my dad. He's coming to the wedding."

Janina threw her arms around him. "That's wonderful. When will he get here?"

"He's flying into San Jose at eleven-forty tomorrow night."

"Tomorrow night! That's great. I can't wait to meet him. I wish I had enough room so that he could stay here."

David cocked an eyebrow. "Well, he could have my bed in the den and I'll bunk with you."

"You can't mean that! David, if you think I'm going to let you—"

He started laughing and held up his hands. "Just joking, love. Actually, I thought it might be best if I moved back into the motel until after the wedding. I've already made reservations for both Dad and me at the Presidential starting tomorrow night."

She felt silly and it showed on her face. If she had had her wits about her, she would have realized that David could never have been so insensitive as to embarrass her in front of his father.

She hugged him. "One of these days you're going to push your luck too far, Dr. Madison."

LATER, AS DAVID AND JANINA WERE LOUNGING on a pad on the patio Janina looked over at David and tilted her sunglasses down on her nose. "Where have you been for the past five minutes?"

"Um. Thinking about our latest commando raid. As long as I live I'll never forget the expressions on their faces when you drank the coffee. Clever idea, using the thermos. You had it all planned out ahead of time, didn't you?"

"No. But I knew they would be more willing to cooperate if they thought we still had some of the bacteria in our possession."

"Well, that was some security blanket. It turned the trick."

"It wouldn't have without you there to back me up."

He bent down and kissed her mouth. At first he brushed across her lips as gently as a summer mist, but then his kiss deepened. She moved closer and linked her hands behind his head.

"We're good together, you know that?"

"I know. And not just on commando raids, either. When we set up our clinic down in San Diego, we'll have one of the best preventative medicine facilities in the country. I think we're going to succeed brilliantly at everything we do. Right?"

"Right."

"So what do you want to do now?" There was an unmistakable leer in his voice.

She looked up innocently. "Now that you ask... I never did get the bedroom painted. Maybe we could start on that before time to go up to the hospital to see Debbie."

His eyes smoldered as he gazed at her. "You've learned to tempt fate these past few weeks. I hope you're ready to pay the price."

He grabbed her shoulders and covered her mouth in a hot, demanding kiss that drained her of all her control. She rolled over against him in a well-calculated move that sent torrents of passion rushing through her body.

Janina felt his instant response. He moved on top of her and again found her mouth and began kissing her in an agony of desire.

"David?"

He pulled away reluctantly, his voice husky and intense. "I hope you aren't going to interrupt this for anything less than an atomic war."

"I wouldn't dream of it."

"What then?"

"I was simply going to suggest that we might be more comfortable on the bed. My neighbor has a beeline view of the patio from his second-floor apartment."

David swore softly. "There's something to be said for country living with wide open spaces between houses." He rose from the pad in one fluid motion then reached for her hands and pulled her up. "Shall I carry you?"

"No, you shall not! You'd drop me after the first ten feet. I'm not exactly a lightweight."

He bent down and scooped her up. "And I'm not exactly a weakling. Besides, there is no way I'm letting you get away from me." He pushed open the door with his foot and carried her inside and down the hall to her bedroom.

"Any more comments about my manhood?"

She giggled. "I'll let you know in about an hour... if you hold up that long."

"I love your choice of words." He grinned, then nuzzled her neck.

"I thought you would." Her last words came breathlessly. His breathing, too, had become rapid and intense. He laid her carefully on the bed then knelt there beside her. There was a strange expression on his face and Janina was puzzled.

"What is it, David?"

He shook his head. "I don't know. I've never felt this way before. I love you, Nina. I love you more than I ever dreamed possible."

She leaned up on one elbow and touched his face with her fingertips. "I need you, David. Make love to me."

His eyes filled with moisture and he blinked rapidly. "I didn't think I'd ever hear you say that again. I hope you won't ever stop needing me."

"Never."

She moved over to make room for him and he came down beside her, their bodies molding together from head to foot.

It occurred to her later that David was right. They *were* good together. But she already knew that.

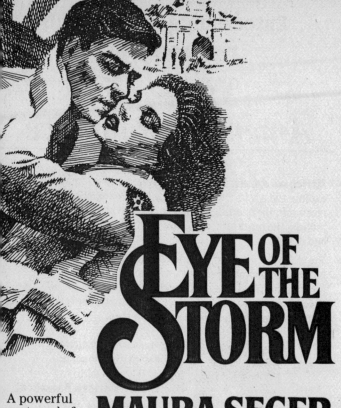

EYE OF THE STORM

MAURA SEGER

A powerful
portrayal of
the events of
World War II in the
Pacific, *Eye of the Storm* is a riveting story of how love
triumphs over hatred. In this, the first of a three book
chronicle, Army nurse Maggie Lawrence meets Marine
Sgt. Anthony Gargano. Despite military regulations
against fraternization, they resolve to face together
whatever lies ahead.... Also known by her fans as
Laurel Winslow, Sara Jennings, Anne MacNeil and
Jenny Bates, Maura Seger, author of this searing novel,
was named by ROMANTIC TIMES as 1984's Most
Versatile Romance Author.

At your favorite bookstore in March.

Get this book FREE!

Mail to:

Harlequin Reader Service

In the U.S.
2504 West Southern Ave.
Tempe, AZ 85282

In Canada
P.O. Box 2800, Postal Station A
5170 Yonge St., Willowdale, Ont. M2N 5T5

YES! I want to be one of the first to discover **Harlequin American Romance.** Send me FREE and without obligation *Twice in a Lifetime.* If you do not hear from me after I have examined my FREE book, please send me the 4 new **Harlequin American Romances** each month as soon as they come off the presses. I understand that I will be billed only $2.25 for each book (total $9.00). There are no shipping or handling charges. There is no minimum number of books that I have to purchase. In fact, I may cancel this arrangement at any time. *Twice in a Lifetime* is mine to keep as a FREE gift, even if I do not buy any additional books.

Name _____ (please print)

Address _____ Apt. no.

City _____ State/Prov. _____ Zip/Postal Code

Signature (If under 18, parent or guardian must sign.)